Caffeine Ni[...]

Medium Wave

Rose Zolock

Fiction to die for…

Published by Caffeine Nights Publishing 2018

Copyright © Rose Zolock 2018

Rose Zolock has asserted her right under the Copyright, Designs and Patents Act 1998 to be identified as the author of this work.

CONDITIONS OF SALE

All rights reserved. No part of this publication may be reproduced, stored in a retrieval system, or transmitted in any form or by any means, electronic, mechanical, photocopying, scanning, recording or otherwise, without the prior permission of the publisher.

This book has been sold subject to the condition that it shall not, by way of trade or otherwise, be lent, resold, hired out, or otherwise circulated without the publisher's prior consent in any form of binding or cover other than that in which it is published and without a similar condition including this condition being imposed on the subsequent purchaser.

All characters in this publication are fictitious and any resemblance to real persons, living or dead is purely coincidental.

Published in Great Britain by
Caffeine Nights Publishing
4 Eton Close
Walderslade
Chatham
Kent
ME5 9AT

www.caffeinenights.com

British Library Cataloguing in Publication Data.
A CIP catalogue record for this book is available from the British Library

ISBN: 978-1-910720-08-0

Also available as an eBook

Cover design by
Mark (Wills) Williams

Everything else by
Default, Luck and Accident

Early reviews for Medium Wave

"Some pages virtually dripped with menace and atmosphere" Brian Callar

A dark and foreboding story and one you will want to read with the lights well and truly turned on! Sarah Hardy

For my mother, Susan
and my grandmother, Marion

MEDIUM WAVE

A PARANORMAL JOURNEY

CHAPTER ONE

The radio studio was dimly lit.

Becky Moran was sitting alone in the darkened space, broadcasting live. Her headphones had pushed her long, dark red hair away from her face and her profile was in shadow, the glow of a computer screen sculpting the curves of her face. On the table in front of her, just within the reach of her hand, lay one of the most controversial paranormal baubles in history.

Becky's voice was clearly amplified in her headphones; she began to speak.

'I am about to touch a piece of supernatural history. Four hundred years old, this was the crystal of Dr John Dee.' Becky's voice was low and mellifluous into the black foam-covered microphone. 'Very few have ever had the opportunity to touch this artefact, but I have special permission to share this experience with you.' Becky knew her audience was waiting, wanting to hear what would happen. She was aware of every phone line into the studio flashing red on the console in front of her. 'Dr John Dee, known to history as the Queen's Magician, was a powerful alchemist and was the Royal Astronomer to Elizabeth the First. It was said that she never made a major decision without his divination.' Becky's hand moved towards the crystal. She had been anticipating this moment for a long time; her pale face flushed slightly – she wanted to touch it, feel it, to share this experience with her listeners. 'Dr John Dee was a Renaissance man in Tudor England. He combined science with magic, he challenged religion, and he revered the supernatural. Think of his work, if you will, as a battle between God and the Devil. He was a powerful, venerated, and mysterious magician. His crystal has a dark and fascinating story to tell...'

The crimson light from the illuminated *'On Air'* logo bathed the purple-tinged quartz with strange shadows. As Becky had been speaking, it appeared to be glittering, flawless, and clear, and then it had faded to a milky opacity. The orb – not large, it could have sat in the palm of a hand – was encircled by an ornate ribbon of silver, thin and shaped into layered, engraved leaves that cupped the outer rim in a cradle, framing the smooth roundness of the quartz. A solid bevel held a silver chain, allowing the crystal to be held, suspended in the air. The ribbon, that strip of antique, worn metal wrapped around the globe, was secured by three tiny pins of silver. The ancient stone was held in a perfect circle, framed to the air and to the light.

Becky's fingers reached closer to the black velvet cushion where John Dee's crystal lay waiting. The silver chain was dull and mottled, and she could smell ancient metal, acrid and pungent, almost sickly sweet. Becky wrinkled her nose as she grasped the chain to hold up the relic, admiring its weight and symmetry. Her finger could just slide through the larger silver loop at the top. She felt the cool, worn, ancient metal as it slipped smoothly over her forefinger. She smiled with pleasure to be able, at last, to hold this piece of paranormal history. It had taken months of negotiation with the Science Museum in London to allow Becky to handle it. She looked up at her production team in the next room, soundproofed behind the glass wall, who were watching, entranced, as Becky Moran lifted the artefact. Her producer, Olly, gave her a thumbs-up of encouragement. Olly was dark-haired, a tall man with an open face. Becky relied on him a great deal and she admired his ability to combine his ambition with creativity. He always made her feel safe – in control – during her live broadcasts. Becky smiled at Olly, a smile of reassurance, and turned her attention back to the crystal.

'What we do know about this particular supernatural relic is that the Elizabethan occult magician, Dr John Dee, wore this crystal on a chain, threaded on a piece of black cord, around his neck. We have to imagine that it was able to explore other worlds, other dimensions. I like to think of it weighted around his neck, swathed and wrapped inside his flowing black robes. No one knows where this bauble came from. His enemies said it was born of occult practice, his admirers and believers said it came from the angels – this drop of ancient crystal.'

Becky glanced at the computer screen in front of her, looking at her script and the research notes prepared by her production team. However, what everyone listening really wanted to know was what would happen when Becky touched the crystal, this relic which Elizabeth the First had been convinced could connect with other worlds.

'This is a talisman which influenced history – the crystal of the Queen's Magician,' Becky said slowly, to emphasise the significance of the moment. 'This talisman is said to heal the sick. The claim was that it allows the angels to speak to us and – most powerfully – it is said to summon the dead.'

The twenty-first-century psychic, Becky Moran, continued to describe the sixteenth-century quartz, her voice soft and beguiling as she broadcast her live weekly radio show *Medium Wave*, which was networked throughout Britain and streamed online to an international audience. The ratings were huge, Becky's listeners enthralled by her encounters with the unexplained and the spirit world. They listened to a woman they trusted and believed in, a woman they felt they knew. Becky Moran spoke directly to them, and she also appeared to speak directly to the dead each week, interviewing many willing to tell their stories of the supernatural.

Becky's show was broadcast on the national talk station 'Voice of Britain'. The station's building was an impressive glass cube located in London's Covent Garden. The outer walls were pale-green glass, which reflected the light. The exposed steel struts were painted to look like stone. The presenters and their production teams were clearly visible on the ground floor, broadcasting to the nation, while the external upper glass walls were embossed with photographs of the presenters. The Voice of Britain logo ran along the external length of the top floor: a British bulldog in front of a radio microphone. They had stopped just short of adding neon lights. This was the UK's premier news and talk radio station.

The microphone and the table at which Becky was sitting were clearly visible from outside the Cube. Subtle uplighting illuminated the studio. Anyone outside – though no one was lingering this Friday evening in the pouring rain – could peer in and see the programme being broadcast. If anyone had been standing just outside the raised security bollards on the pavement that night, they would have seen a beautiful redhead in her early thirties, wearing her signature black dress, worn slightly off the shoulder. Her black Louboutin shoes with the red soles were, as usual, kicked off for the broadcast. Becky's head was bowed towards the microphone.

She took her eyes away from the artefact for a second and looked up at the green glass wall, water running down the outside, smudging the street and smearing the lights glowing from the passing traffic and streetlamps. London seemed tinged with a pale-green colour wash, remote and unfocused. Calm and peaceful; it was a watery curtain from reality.

Becky reached for the stone. It was dark, waiting, cushioned on the black velvet, absorbing the red electric light that swirled within its depths, casting a deep pall.

As she lifted the chain it swung slightly, the quartz swaying at her eye level, suspended in the subdued light of the radio studio. 'I have the chain looped on my finger and I can tell you I can smell the antique metal – it smells sweet and musty – and the crystal? Well, it is cool to my touch. I am cupping the stone in my hand now. It is heavy and it is cold.'

Becky felt the weight of the quartz; the smooth surface seemed to slide in her hand as if she were holding a perfect round of ice wrapped in that ribbon of metal. 'This feels to me as if who – or whatever – polished this stone had the ability, long before modern machines were invented, to make sure the crystal would last through time. I can tell you it feels heavier than I thought it would. It's quite remarkable that I hold in my hand an object Queen Elizabeth the First knew so well.' Becky wrapped her fingers around the stone, so it was encased firmly in her hand.

'I can sense a power here,' she said quietly. Her eyes closed as she felt a slight shudder run into her palm. 'I can feel something here, as I hold it in my hand. Not quite a vibration.' Becky searched for the words to describe what she was feeling. 'More a sense that the stone has power deep inside it.' Disconcerted, Becky paused and unfurled her hand, feeling very strongly she did not want to hold Dr John Dee's crystal for much longer. She lifted the orb once more on the chain, sliding the sliver loop back over her finger. She peered at the artefact, a small frown on her forehead, her grey eyes narrowing slightly. 'I am looking into the quartz now, holding it just in front of my eyes and I can see a glittering – some refracted crimson light – no, wait, now it's like a shaft of white light.' Becky's voice, which had been mesmeric, was now surprised, startled as she stared at the object swinging, spellbinding, in front of her face. She knew she had to broadcast her experience, keep her audience with her as she told this story. She glanced at her notes and steadied herself.

'If I look deeply, if I concentrate, will I see what Dr John Dee saw? Deep in this crystal – will I see whatever made him cross the boundary between God and science and into... magic?'

Becky leaned into the microphone as if to talk more intimately with her audience. She paused again, aware they were waiting, expectantly, for some supernatural revelation.

'Now I can see wisps of red light swirling inside this antiquated quartz. As I talk to you, the crystal is swinging hypnotically, side to side from the silver chain. I am not moving my hand or making it move in any way.' Indeed, Becky's hand was steady as she balanced the stone from her finger. She frowned deeply, puzzled as to why the crystal was swinging like a pendulum. She glanced up at her team who were transfixed by the quartz hanging off her finger, watching her broadcast from the Ops centre through the internal glass wall that divided them. She looked again at the stone. 'I can see...' She stopped speaking.

For the briefest moment, the dim lights in the radio studio began to flicker. Becky Moran saw the swirling light within the crystal fade, bleaching the quartz to a dried husk, the colour of an empty wasps' nest. The stone stopped swinging and, alarmed, she almost dropped the chain from her fingers, until she realised that it must be – it had to be – just a trick of the light.

Her voice had been steady and sure but now came across as uncertain and afraid. She leant back, slightly away from her microphone. 'The quartz has stopped moving – the colour of the stone has completely changed...' For a moment, all Becky could see was the crystal, now a crinkled shell, a globule of yellow-tinged, rotten rock, swinging suspended in darkness. She blinked, sure the metal loop on her finger had become icy cold.

She heard a click in her headphones, as Olly, who had been watching her closely through the glass, pressed his talkback button. He was clearly alarmed, aware that Becky had been silent for several seconds.

Becky glanced up and nodded a visual 'thank you' towards her producer for bringing her attention back to the radio studio. She knew she was still on air and that she had to recover quickly. She felt displaced, not an experience she was familiar with. She was usually so sure of what she was doing, knowing what her listeners wanted from her, able to deliver it. It was as if this reality had dissipated for a while and all there had been was the crystal, suspended in the dim lighting, emanating a power that blocked out the reality of Becky Moran and her stories of the supernatural and the strange.

Intellectually, Becky was astute enough to realise that the modern desire to believe in magic and a psychic ability to communicate with the dead was, in fact, very similar to that of the Elizabethans. For a while, the world really believed that Dr John Dee could see and talk to another dimension. Becky had thought before she touched his crystal, that even he probably believed it. Now, she actually felt afraid. Nothing had ever spooked Becky Moran before. She was hailed as a modern-day psychic medium. She had her own radio show, she was about to start filming a pilot for a TV series, she filled theatres with people wanting to hear from the departed, and many came for expensive one-on-one readings. Becky reassured the grieving by gently placing her hand on their arm, comforting and sincere. All that, combined with her lucrative website, ensured that Becky was famous for her supernatural powers.

But Becky Moran was not all she seemed. For the most part, she was a constructed show business act and broadcaster, cleverly fooling the world into believing she had clairvoyant power. It sometimes made her feel guilty, but it had also made her famous and wealthy. She had learned to live with the art of deception. Whilst she had always had a strong intuition about people, a sixth sense she could not explain, her so-called psychic powers were a myth.

Put simply, Becky Moran was a fake – and a good one.

For her to experience some trickery of the light in the radio studio with a piece of history – clearly that was just ridiculous. Becky tried to rationalise what was happening to her, her mind struggling to make sense of it. Yet she was frightened – yes, that was what it was – a real sense of fear. As she realised that, she became aware she was still silent and still on air. Olly buzzed again in her ear. 'Becky?'

She mentally shook the fear away and focused again on the object, which was still looped on her finger, now perfectly still on the silver chain. She leaned again towards the microphone.

'Dr Dee's stone has stopped swinging – the lights flickered in here – I think we had a power surge here at The Voice of Britain.' Becky tried not to sound uncertain.

'For a moment the crystal seemed drained of all colour. In fact, it looked dried out, empty, sinister. I can't explain it and it threw me for a second, I will be honest with you. I do sense a power here.'

Becky was regaining control as she looked again at the stone, which now looked dead. Nothing more than a black pebble wrapped in ancient silver.

'I am replacing this ancient artefact back on the velvet cushion.' She put it down, resisting the urge to wipe her hand where it had touched the stone. She flexed her fingers outwards as if to shake off the stain she felt was smeared on her palm, to cleanse off the rank odour of the metal.

'*Medium Wave* wants to thank the Science Museum here in London for allowing us to examine the crystal of Dr John Dee. It leaves for America next week to be part of a special touring exhibition of historic occult items from Elizabethan England. This artefact will go back on display in the museum in its secure glass case until then.

'Perhaps that is the best place for it.

'*Medium Wave* will be back right after this.'

The red *On Air* light clicked off as the radio station played out a commercial break.

Becky sat back in her chair, confused and shaken by what had just happened with Dr John Dee's crystal. She was reluctant to touch it again, pushing the black velvet cushion away from her. The stone looked completely dead and lifeless.

Olly Harvey, Becky's producer, was watching her from the Ops centre. He had been admiring her telling of the story of John

Dee's crystal, her words painting the picture of the object, the build-up of suspense before she touched it. He had one eye on the incoming phone lines where he was anticipating a slew of callers who believed in all this paranormal wackjob nonsense and would want to tell their own stories of the strange. Olly knew their dedicated audience would love this Elizabethan bauble. He had negotiated hard with the Science Museum to allow Becky to handle it, and he smiled as he remembered the promise that it would be treated with respect. He knew Becky would honour that promise and he had briefed her well. His smile widened as the switchboard in front of him flashed like a slot machine.

However, as Olly watched and listened, Becky had begun to falter as she held the crystal in her hand; she was sounding strange, somehow off-kilter, and he was alarmed. He knew Becky was a constructed act and a good one. His own hand moved to hover over the talkback button and he stared hard through the glass, his eyes narrowing with concern. His presenter was usually so sure-footed and convincing in the world of the paranormal, which Olly had no time for. Week after week, he set up guests for Becky which challenged his rational mind. Olly's journey into the land of the strange made him feel that the world was filled with the gullible, all of them searching for some supernatural reassurance. He often reminded himself that back home in Sunderland, his dad would be having a pint and the friends he grew up with, played rugby with, was living in a world that had nothing to do with paranormal baubles.

Olly knew entertainment was entertainment and his passion was making great programmes – even if the subject matter was bordering on the ridiculous. He had looked on John Dee's crystal as a historic artefact sitting in a museum. Nothing more, nothing less. He had kept those thoughts to himself as Becky had reached her hand out towards it. Olly was captivated by her narrative, smiling in admiration as she crafted the story behind it.

But, as she hesitated, Olly's head snapped away from the flashing lights on the phone console and he looked to see what was wrong with Becky. She was holding the crystal, her voice faltering into the microphone, and he saw her face twist with what looked like fear; she was pale. Olly found this hard to understand. He wondered if she was ill – he had to focus on keeping her on track. Olly never usually had to click the talkback button to shape her performance and he knew something was wrong. Olly then watched Becky push the crystal away and he felt an adrenalin rush in his stomach, alarmed at her reaction.

'You okay, Becky?' Olly leaned towards the glass as he pressed the talkback button, looking directly at her.

She looked up and silently nodded at him through the glass. Her expression was confident, and Olly smiled, feeling relieved. He mentally shook his head and rationalised the last few minutes were just a blip, a bit of drama. All he wanted was for Becky and *Medium Wave* to run smoothly, and they were live on air. The programme had to come first. 'Well done, the phone lines are going mad in here – they want to know you are okay. Reassure them and let's move on,' he told her. 'Two minutes on the ad break.'

Sarah Jones pushed through the studio door, carrying a glass of iced water and leading the Science Museum security man inside. She walked up to Becky, feeling anxious concern as she half smiled, seeking reassurance.

'Are you all right?' she asked her. 'You seemed a bit thrown by that thing.' Sarah jerked her head towards the crystal, a dark stone now looking very ordinary on the black velvet cushion. Sarah heard and felt her dangling ebony and silver earrings clanking as she swung her head. She put the glass on the table by the microphone, her red kaftan wafting a musty aroma. Sarah was proud to be Becky's assistant, and she also acted as a runner on Friday nights, when *Medium Wave* was broadcast. She ran the hospitality for the guests in the Green Room and then packed them off in a taxi when their interviews were over. Tonight, was a busy night and Sarah knew she had much to do. Her main job right now, though, was making sure Becky had everything she needed.

Sarah was third generation Black British, large and flamboyant; she loved charity shops and would have been astonished if anyone had told her there was a smell of mothballs which lingered on her vintage clothes. Sarah thought her style totally 'boho' and a tribute to her heritage. She watched as the security guard began to pack away the crystal in a steel box. Her fingers flexed as she longed to touch it, but there wasn't time before the red light clicked on and the programme was live again. Besides, she was a little afraid of it. Dr John Dee's crystal fascinated her and she was more than intrigued by Becky's unusual reaction to it. Sarah believed Becky did have a gift, despite knowing that she and the *Medium Wave* team worked hard to construct this programme about the paranormal.

Becky reached over and rested her hand briefly on Sarah's arm as they both watched the crystal being packed away. It was a touch of gratitude and Sarah felt reassured. Becky looked up at Sarah from her seat at the microphone. 'Yes, thanks – it just spooked me a little. I wouldn't want to be on the plane when they fly that thing over to New York.' Becky flexed her shoulders as if to shake off the power of the crystal. It was almost a shudder as she looked up at Sarah. 'Just a supernatural rock, after all.'

Sarah was surprised. Becky was usually so calm and collected; nothing ever seemed to faze her. 'It sounded great, Becky. Anything else you need?' Becky shook her head and it crossed Sarah's mind that her friend may truly have been spooked. Sarah felt a need to protect this woman, who always looked so fragile, and felt strongly that the object in the steel case had to be gone. She tried to hide her concern, smiled at Becky again, and then turned to get the security man, who was now carrying Dr John Dee's bauble hidden away in the box, to the studio door as fast as possible. He walked in front of her, holding the box in his arms.

Sarah paused at the door, seeing Becky's head bent, flicking at her computer screen, her face illuminated. Sarah had to dismiss the thought that Becky looked isolated in here, all alone. She turned, calling back over her shoulder through the door she held open with one hand. 'I'm bringing the ghost hunting vicar in next,' she said as she closed the studio door behind her.

Becky glanced at the clock and calculated she had about a minute before she would have to continue with the show.

The studio door opened again and Hugh Jolly, her business partner at their production company, Divine Diva, put his head around the door. Becky looked at the man who had shaped this deception, this persona of Becky Moran, and created the mystique of his psychic star. He was immaculate in Gucci. 'I am a Gucci whore and proud of it!' he had told Becky ten years ago at their first meeting when Becky was a student at Cambridge University. Hugh was now in his fifties, still slim, tall, and spruced up for a date later with a young actor fresh from RADA after *Medium Wave* went off air at midnight.

'What happened there?' he asked. 'Did old Doc Dee spook you?' He grinned at Becky. 'Cracking item, that, well done spooking it up. Just the right amount of drama. I love it when you sound frightened.'

'Did you see the stone change colour? When the light flickered?' Becky was sharp, aware that the *On Air* light was about to click back on.

'Don't be silly, darling,' Hugh said soothingly, still smiling. 'You're starting to sound like a punter. All that little segment needed was you spewing up some ectoplasm and then we would have heard rapping on the table.' Hugh knocked his fist on the wooden edge of the door as he twisted his face in faux terror, then he threw back his head and laughed loudly. 'Well done, though. Even I believed something just happened there.'

Becky felt a flash of annoyance with Hugh for being so flippant. She was still frightened, and stressed, aware she was about to be live on air and the seconds were ticking. She stared at him, clearly indicating he should go. He stepped back, his floppy hair bouncing over his aquiline face as it became apparent Becky wasn't in the mood. The studio door closed behind him.

Becky felt cold, disturbed by the illusion the light had caused on Dr John Dee's crystal. That had been the first item on tonight's show. As the final commercial ran ('Thirty seconds,' buzzed Olly in her ear), she sipped on the glass of iced water, gathered her thoughts, and quickly read through the rest of the running order for tonight's show. The guests included a Church of England vicar who wore black leather and saw ghosts for a living, and a woman from Aberdeen who called herself 'Whisper', who claimed that in her past life she'd been Merlin's mistress and had had sex with King Arthur on the Round Table. The star turn tonight, however, was an American called John X, who claimed to be ex-CIA, trained in remote viewing, and a so-called psychic spy. Becky knew he was recovering from a breakdown – he had been sectioned for a while. He was going to be flogging a book that night in which he claimed to have seen the Ark of the Covenant and knew exactly where it was.

Then there were the phone readings she would do, displaying the mediumship that had made her famous. The callers were all set up and researched by her Divine Diva radio production team. Whilst *Medium Wave* invited callers on to the show to talk to Becky for a reading, those who appeared on air were set-ups. Becky had a full brief (thanks to Sarah, who did the research) about the caller, who they had lost, and some other details with which she could amaze the public in an on-air reading. There was nothing spontaneous on *Medium Wave* at all. Until now.

Becky tried to shake off the strange experience with John Dee's crystal and smiled as she pictured her mother's soirée in Leeds, where broccoli quiche and Prosecco would be being served. Every Friday, Iris invited her friends around, so they could listen to Becky's show. Iris loved her daughter's celebrity. Her father, Peter, always went out. He loathed Becky's chosen career; he knew it was a sham and believed it a total waste of a degree from Cambridge.

It was twenty-one minutes past ten. Becky glanced up at the digital clock in her radio studio, totally unaware her entire world was about to change.

CHAPTER TWO

Becky tapped at her keyboard, headphones on, waiting for the commercial break to end and the red light to snap back on. She wrinkled her face as she became aware of an unpleasant smell. She stopped tapping.

The smell of decay was getting stronger.

She looked up and glanced into the Ops room at the technician, Nick, who drove the desk and digital computers, controlling everything that went on air. Becky could see he was absorbed in his screens, setting up the jingles for her programme. He did not look as if he had noticed a bad smell. Olly was talking to Hugh, his back to her, and Hugh was laughing, as if at some dirty joke. Becky became aware that the already dim mood lighting of the studio was darkening.

Becky felt as though she had slipped into a room that looked like her studio but was not.

She was aware of a low hum. Indistinct, it was more like a vibration. A steady pulse. She pushed herself away from the table and slipped her headphones off. The sound did not change, it thrummed as if from far away, almost indistinct. She could feel it, however, in her bones, in the very tissue of her flesh. Even the webbing between her fingers seemed to feel it. Becky looked at her hands.

The table she was sitting at seemed more starkly outlined, almost as if she were looking at a black and white picture instead of colour and substance. Even the glass of iced water looked monochrome, and the flashing lights on the console – each light a caller in to her show – were pulsing with a dirty glow. This did not make any sense. The microphone had also altered. It was in the same place, at the same angle, but now looking sinister, as if it may raise itself up like a cobra and attack.

Becky pushed herself further away from the table. The uplighting was now much dimmed and, far from being warm, the light was tinged red and throbbed. As she heard the low steady hum, she felt the sound reaching her solar plexus, and thought that as the hum became more profound, resonating, the light seemed connected to it, deepening and flickering with the vibration.

Becky was reminded of the sound made by a dentist's drill, grinding inside your head, reverberating.

The smell was getting worse. Becky's mouth was dry; the taste of decay filled her nostrils and her mouth. She looked down. As ever when she was broadcasting, Becky's Louboutins were discarded by her chair, but the thin grey carpet appeared to be shifting, rippling, and moving to the pitch of that reverberation, like incoming waves on a shingle beach. She lifted her feet instinctively. As she did so, she was sure that, out of the corner of her eye, something moved just over by the door. Something that looked like a hand, reaching up through the carpet, stretching the fabric and then swiftly moving back down below. Becky made a small noise of fear.

She looked up at the walls. The logo had gone. The soundproofing fabric was moving. Or Becky thought it was. That red glow made it hard to see clearly. As she looked, her heart racing, the taste of decay filling her mouth, Becky saw faces pressing through from the other side of the fabric, faces contorted as if they were screaming in agony before then being yanked away. Everything in the studio was now changing almost imperceptibly, shape-shifting. The edge of the table near her right hand was softening, appearing to meld into deep blood-red ripples, with blobs dripping slowly down like wax on a pillar candle. The microphone became ever more serpentine. She twisted on her chair as it softened and sank downwards, and was aware that the indistinct thrum, thrum was getting louder, deeper, grinding into her body.

Then she looked towards the outside, at the glass wall, and her flesh crawled. Adrenalin pumped into her system; she opened her mouth to scream, unable to move from the chair with her feet lifted away from the shifting floor. Standing outside, silhouetted in the now red glow and framed by the rain running down the window, were dark shapes, indistinct dark shapes, like solid shadows, with no faces, their body mass pressing into the glass.

The thrum, thrum, thrum became louder and Becky now heard something else: a chorus of voices, voices that rumbled and moaned and were building to a crescendo, a sound of blackness, of dirt, of the grave – inhuman voices; she could hear them.

'We are here,' they said, the sound twisting itself into the thrum, thrum of the dark rhythm.

Then the lights went out.

The blackness was total. Becky Moran was absorbed by it. For a second, there was nothing. No breath, no sound, no heartbeat, no sense, no touch – just suspension without connection to the physical world. It was as if she and that darkness were one. She could see nothing. She was not aware of the seat beneath her. Her fear erased her logical thought processes.

They say that fear, when it comes, takes many forms. It could be that moment when the doctor in his white coat, his eyes kind with sympathy, tells you that they cannot operate. Or the adulterer's fear when the deception is finally unmasked. The fear of answering the door to a police officer who may have news of a fatal accident. That of growing old and being alone. The fear of failure. The terror of a child who is convinced that an ancient hand, green with decay and with long, curling nails encrusted with the dirt of the coffin will wrap itself around her bare ankle when she puts her foot on the cold floor. There are the new, twenty-first century fears of jet planes exploding, of a suicide bomber on your crowded Tube carriage, of a deadly virus breeding silently in the city centre. Fears, real and imagined, which shape behaviour and change lives as human beings try to get through their short span of time on Earth.

For Becky Moran, her fear at that moment transcended the external. It was internal. It wrapped itself inside her body, winding through her bones and muscles, twisting itself around her brain and coiling under her skin.

The thrum, thrum, thrum had ceased. No sound vibrated around her now and it was as if the air itself had gone, swallowed up by the darkness. The voices were silenced. In that black vacuum, the collection of cells and DNA which made up Becky

Moran were absorbed into an infinite mass of the nebulous. It was as if her existence had almost been eradicated.

She inhaled sharply, and the returning air, as it passed through her mouth and into her lungs, jolted Becky back to some level of perception. Now she could hear her heartbeat, fast and loud, banging steadily in its own terrified rhythm. She knew her eyes were open, but there was no light, no light. Her breath, now recovered, was shallow and rapid. She was unable to move, even though she was not aware of anything binding her limbs. Yet she was more conscious of her body, even the feel of the fabric of her dress, scratchy on her skin, of her bare feet, and even the weight of her hair on her shoulders.

Her brain tried to work out why she had been enveloped by this oppressive blackness; fear jiggled the synapses to snap from a dream-like state to a panic response because this environment – this experience – made no sense.

Seconds had passed since the lights went out, but Becky felt as though this isolation in the dark had always been. Ahead of her, a pinpoint of white light – very far away – pierced the blackness. Becky focused her eyes towards it as it grew wider, larger and nearer. She sensed the darkness fighting that light, a heaviness around her pushing at it, a strong unseen force wanting to flatten that light, eradicate it, conquer it, and end it.

It was a pure light. Becky wanted it, wanted that illumination, and knew that within it lay escape, salvation, safety. Her stomach muscles tightened as she bent, leant towards that white light, now bigger and brighter and winning over the dark mass. Her arm reached towards it and, as she moved, the darkness expanded around her in one last attempt to swallow her, make her a part of it without end, suck her into it, absorb her existence and own her.

But the light expanded towards her and Becky moaned with longing, a desperate sound, a sound of gratitude that spoke of survival, hope, and redemption. As the light reached her body and bathed her, a voice as black as that diminishing darkness whispered:

'We are here.'

In the moments before the darkness, Nick, the technician, had looked up to see Becky Moran push herself back from the microphone and take her headphones off. He was just about to turn and tell Olly, who was sitting near him and taking a call from a listener at his console in the Ops room. As he looked towards Olly, Nick's hand instinctively went to buzz Becky in her headphones to ask if she was all right, when the electricity in the whole building, including his digital desk and every computer system and every light, went off.

'Fuck,' said Nick.

'Fuck!' echoed Olly.

'What the fuck?' asked Hugh.

Sitting in total darkness, Nick was blinking fast and trying to work out what was happening. He knew power failures at broadcast centres such as The Voice of Britain were dealt with by an immediate default to a generator; failing that, battery-powered systems kicked in until the fault was fixed. A total failure was unheard of. Nick began to panic. In the darkness, he couldn't think quickly enough. Why were none of the back-up systems kicking in? As he struggled for some light, he remembered the only thing which could cause a total blackout: a lightning strike. Nick's heart was beating very fast as he reached for the phone to track down an engineer.

Upstairs, on the first floor of the Cube, Sarah was in the Green Room when the lights went out. There was confusion. She could see a dark shape, which was John X in a foetal position, rocking in the darkness, mumbling that he was sorry, so sorry, and then screaming that God would punish all of them. Sarah started to move and stumbled over the black leather-clad leg of the vicar who was trying to comfort the American by saying the Lord's Prayer.

'Shift, will you?' said Sarah. 'The power is off.' The vicar apologised as Sarah pushed past him, feeling her way in the darkness in an attempt to get to the door. She could see the lights were off in the street outside and, as she looked towards the window, she could make out the silhouette of Whisper, the past-life queen, standing by the glass wall and looking out.

'Merlin will fix it,' she said dreamily as Sarah finally found and opened the Green Room door.

'Oh, he's an electrician, is he?' Sarah snapped, inching out into the corridor in the dark towards the emergency staircase, lit by a fluorescent EXIT sign. She needed to get downstairs to see Hugh and find out what was happening.

In the seconds after the complete power failure, Olly held up his mobile phone to get some light. He could see that the power was out on the street too. Nick was frantically pressing buttons and trying to call the station's chief engineer because he couldn't even put the station on to the emergency tape, which was normal practice if there was a fire alarm or bomb scare. He looked at his control desk as if it were an unfaithful woman who had betrayed his love and devotion.

'Can't do anything, mate,' he said to Hugh Jolly, who was now swigging from the hip flask he kept in the inside pocket of the Gucci suit, and looking very annoyed in the glow of Olly's iPhone torch.

'Try,' said Hugh.

'I am trying.'

'Try fucking harder,' said Hugh, between swallows.

Two minutes had passed since the power went off, and Olly edged his way to the door to go and check on Becky. His iPhone sent an arc of light into the darkness. He pushed open the door to her studio and shone the torch into the room. The light flooded the darkness and reflected off the glass wall that faced the street. Becky Moran was sitting just where he had seen her a few minutes before, her head in her hands, bent forward in her chair. He thought she was sobbing.

'Becky? You all right? It's just a power cut, love. Becky?'

In the eerie glow, Becky Moran raised her head and Olly stepped back in shock. Her face was cast in deep shadows, tears were running down her cheeks, and she was paler than he had ever seen her. However, it was her look of total fear that would haunt Olly for years afterwards. There were deep ridges of fear on that lovely face as she blinked at his light.

'They are here,' she said, gulping the words out and using the back of her hand to wipe her face. 'Didn't you see them?'

Olly came and knelt at her side, putting his arm around her. 'Becky, it's just a power cut. The engineers are on it. What are you talking about? There's no one here but us. Come on, love.'

'No!' Becky pushed him away. 'That darkness, that smell. Didn't you see it? Didn't you hear them? They are here.' Her eyes darted around the darkened recesses of the studio. 'They were outside,' she said, pointing at the glass wall, 'trying to get in. Then... then...' Becky started to sob again. 'The darkness, dear God, that darkness...' She looked at Olly. He held the torch away from her face. 'You must have seen the light? That light? It came to save me.'

Olly was now seriously worried. This wasn't the calm, composed Becky Moran he knew. They had been working together for a year and he had never seen her cry or even get mildly hysterical,

but now he was looking at a terrified woman. He hoped Hugh would come in. 'There's no one here, love.' Olly's Sunderland accent was heavy as he tried to comfort her. 'Honestly, it's just a power cut and they are sorting it. We are off air. You just had a scare.'

He watched Becky stare down at her hands. They were shaking.

By now Hugh had lit his own phone torch and was watching the two of them through the glass from Ops. He wondered what they were doing, why Becky seemed upset. It was like watching a shadow play. He put the hip flask away and lit his way into the studio. As he opened the door, he got a whiff of Sarah's kaftan. He called her 'the mouldy one'; no amount of dry cleaning ever got rid of the waft of mothballs from her second-hand clothes.

'It's a power cut, Sarah,' he said.

'No shit, Sherlock. I have three lunatics in the Green Room praying for salvation. When will they fix it?' she asked, pushing past him. Hugh wrinkled his nose, ignored her and let her go into Ops and have a go at Nick, since he had got nowhere. As he walked into the studio, Hugh saw Becky on the chair with Olly kneeling at her side. The softly illuminated image looked almost like something Goya would have painted. Hugh had to shake off that feeling of the surreal.

'What the fuck is going on?' he said as he stepped forward. But as Becky looked up, even Hugh, with three swallows of vodka and a temper on him because of the power failure, was shocked. 'Christ, Becky, what is it?'

Olly looked at Hugh and shook his head. 'She says someone was here, it was dark, then something about a light...' As Olly spoke, Becky's hand snapped up and grabbed his arm in a violent parody of her trademark human touch.

'Something happened here,' she said. 'Everything has changed.' Then she dropped her head and sobbed.

Hugh cancelled his date with the young actor from RADA and put Becky Moran in a cab. He took her back to his flat overlooking Green Park and wrapped her in a blanket. She looked diminished. She hadn't spoken a word since that outburst with Olly and had offered no resistance to being bundled out of the Cube. Hugh had also despatched Sarah without any hint that there was a crisis going on, and Olly had stayed, after being told to keep his mouth shut and to finish off his work in the production office.

Hugh knew when someone was in shock. He gave Becky hot, sweet tea (whilst himself gulping vodka in his kitchen as he waited for the kettle to boil), kept her warm, and then sat with her on his brown leather Chesterfield sofa, his arm around her, her head resting on his shoulder. He stroked her hair. The fire was lit, casting a soft pall of light and warmth. Hugh made soothing noises and kissed the top of her head from time to time.

The flat in this very expensive part of London came thanks to his legacy from a trust fund, and he had it furnished in the style of a gentlemen's club. He favoured dark, glowing wood, and the walls were lined with books and plays and autobiographies of the theatrical knights. He had stopped short of having a stuffed deer head on the wall, or that signed sketch of Laurence Olivier he'd paid a fortune for when he was flush with cash. That was kept in his bedroom. Soft light also flowed from burnished brass lamps. It was a masculine room and Hugh thought it complemented his public image well.

There were no family photographs anywhere in his home. Hugh's family were in the past. He'd enjoyed the education they'd given him, the money they'd left him, the place he occupied in society. But he didn't need pictorial reminders of any of them.

Until Hugh met and created his version of Becky Moran, he had been a failed theatrical producer. Fortunately, he was also independently wealthy thanks to a legacy from his grandmother, which allowed him to indulge the passion for theatre he'd discovered whilst at Cambridge. Ten years ago he had been in his early forties, once tipped by the critics for greatness. However, he'd had a couple of flops, one of them expensive and just off the West End, which meant he was at a loose end when he walked into a party at a Cambridge college and met Becky Moran.

As he soothed Becky, Hugh remembered the first time they had met, almost a decade ago.

'They're all con men,' Hugh had said to her, sloshing a large glass of vodka in one hand, his other hand sweeping back his floppy hair. The party was drinks and a string quartet, with old dons scoffing canapés after missing dinner, and eager students wanting to make contacts and get their grades up. Hugh was there because he still had a home in Cambridge and was a master of networking. He had cornered the redhead at the party, where a mutual friend had introduced Becky as 'the Cambridge Medium'. Hugh had heard of this undergraduate who claimed she could speak to the dead. It amused him; he believed in creating theatrical illusions. If the dead spoke, it would be from under the trapdoor centre stage with an amplifier and a wind machine. He looked at the small frame of this girl with the grey eyes and wondered just how good she was at this clairvoyant illusion.

'Mediums, psychics, eccentrics – it's just end-of-pier stuff. A bad cast list of oddballs with a penchant for bad clothes, bad hair, and predictable patter. Gruesome.'

Becky smiled up at Hugh, those eyes warm and almost flirtatious. 'I have always had what I would call an intuition,' she said, trying to avoid vodka being splashed on her clothes. 'I always know when the phone will ring, often I know who it will be.' She picked up her own drink. 'When I was ten, my grandfather died in the night. I woke up knowing it. Can't explain it. I never said a word – my mother would have had me exorcised, had the vicar round, all of it. It was far better to keep quiet.' She took a sip of her wine.

Hugh gave Becky the same look he gave young actors who wanted a part in his latest production. His eyebrows raised, and he put his head to one side. 'How do you convince anyone that the dead come to you, speak to you?'

She drew him into the corner of the room, away from the string quartet's rendition of obscure Vivaldi, to a place where they could not be overheard. Hugh scooped up a stuffed mushroom from a silver salver balanced on the arm of a passing waiter and held it between his fingers, the full glass of vodka in the other hand.

Becky told Hugh a story of how one night, in her first year as an undergraduate and after a drunken dinner at St John's College, a few friends started to play a game of who could fool whom. Becky discovered a gift for acting out a psychic reading, using what she knew about her friends and faking the messages coming through. That night, she put a shawl on her head and lit candles, keeping in mind the spiritualists of the Edwardian era, conjuring up the dead amidst the chintz. This appealed to her sense of the dramatic and she liked showing off. What surprised her was just how accurate she could be and how her friends reacted to what she told them.

For the rest of her time as an undergraduate, she did her party trick on demand. A bit of research beforehand, a keen eye for detail – what people said to her, what they wore, their narrative, sometimes a touch of that intuition – meant it was easy for her to convince them she was getting messages from the Other Side. What started out as fun led to a reputation around Cambridge that the redheaded English Literature student was indeed able to connect with the dead.

Hugh snorted and put his glass down on a table. 'See, as I said, just pandering to the gullible.' He bit into the canapé.

Becky then asked him if his father had died not speaking to him. Hugh stopped rolling his eyes and being glib. He swallowed the mouthful, picked up his glass, and took a large swig of vodka.

'Your father says he is sorry. He understands now. Does that make sense to you?' asked Becky. She put her hand on Hugh's arm as she looked at him with concern. Hugh swallowed. His father couldn't accept Hugh's sexuality and they had been estranged before his death.

'How do you know anything about my father?' he asked Becky.

'He is right next to you. His hand is on your shoulder. He wants you to know he understands now.' Hugh was now much less self-assured. Becky laughed. 'Got you! I did my homework on you when I knew you were going to be here tonight. I wanted to meet you. You gave an interview to *The Stage* a few years back and talked about your father. I just used what I knew.'

Hugh was shaken but realised, if he had been convinced by this redhead, what potential there could be. He smiled. 'Let's do lunch,' he said. Becky agreed.

He honed her skills in small venues, they built her persona step by step. At first, they planted punters in audiences, so it appeared that Becky was hearing the dead loud and clear. Then they used spies in the foyer to pick up information from the gullible who came clutching a piece of jewellery from dead parents, hoping for a message, talking amongst themselves. When the venues got bigger, Hugh used hidden earpieces and he schooled Becky into a glamorous but simple stage presence which was striking and well lit. Her signature look was a slightly off-the-shoulder black dress and a pair of Louboutin black shoes complete with red soles. She wore no jewellery. Her red hair was smooth and fell onto her shoulders. She looked groomed and in control, but Becky was unsure about the deception and felt guilty. 'Darling,' said Hugh, that hair flopping, 'we just give the people what they want. It's showbiz, and you are very good at it.' They formed a production company based in Cambridge called Divine Diva and the money rolled in. The radio show was billed as 'entertainment', so as not to contravene regulations about peddling the supernatural. This made Hugh laugh. 'They get away with it on *Songs of Praise*,' he used to joke. Becky combined what intuition she had to try and bring some comfort and learned to quell the guilt about the deception. It made her feel good when someone went away comforted, convinced the dead had spoken. It salved her conscience.

Now, ten years later in his upmarket London flat, Hugh knew that when Becky came around a bit she would talk to him. He just hoped she wasn't ill (he ran off a list in his mind: a brain tumour, dementia, viral infection), on drugs (he had a list that could run for about twenty minutes, but he had never seen Becky so much as take a drag on a cigarette), or having a psychotic episode (he dismissed that one, she was more rational than him, and he also knew what depression looked like). He just soothed her, silent and trembling slightly, and wondered what to do next. If she didn't rally he may have to call a doctor. He hoped not. They had a TV pilot to shoot, stage shows coming up, and there was a lot of money invested in this creation known as Becky Moran.

Hugh had grown to like Becky a lot. Sometimes, almost as much as the money they made.

CHAPTER THREE

Eventually, Becky stopped trembling. She sat up and looked at Hugh. He was relieved to see her grey eyes looked clearer. 'Better?' he asked, handing her the cup of sweet tea.

'Hugh,' said Becky, 'it's all changed.'

'Darling, it's fine. You've been working too hard and tonight you just got freaked when the lights went out and...'

Becky put her hand up to Hugh's mouth to quieten him. It was such an intimate gesture, small but effective, that Hugh shut up.

'Your father says he loves you, but he isn't sorry you never spoke again when you told him you are queer. He says he should have beaten it out of you when you were small. He says he feels it was his responsibility, as your father, to make sure you lived a decent life. He watches you. He is disgusted by you. He knows you are an alcoholic and is warning you that, unless you stop, you are going to die.'

Hugh recoiled from Becky.

'He is standing there.' She pointed to a space by the fireplace, where the mock flame flickered in the tiled surround. The room was warm. Hugh shifted uncomfortably on the leather sofa, blinking at Becky. 'He is tall, like you. His hair is similar but darker. He has a limp from falling off a horse called Triumph in a polo match back in 1999, and he rubs his thigh a lot.' Hugh felt cold recognition sink in the pit of his stomach. 'He has been talking to me for the last half hour. He has asked me to get you to describe the rocking horse your uncle made you when you were five. He says there was something engraved under the saddle...'

'Tempus fugit,' whispered Hugh.

'Yes, he says, that's right. It was your uncle's secret message to you. Time flies, Hugh, your father says. And time may be growing short.' Becky's glistening grey eyes looked at Hugh. 'It's changed,' she said.

Hugh gaped at Becky. The first time she did the father trick, all those years ago in Cambridge, he had been convinced enough to see her potential as a kind of freakshow act. Now it was Hugh who felt like a freak, sitting with a redhead he'd thought he knew, on his sofa, who was telling him that his bloody dead swine of a father was in his lounge, talking bloody shite about bloody rocking horses.

'Stop it, Becky.' Hugh stood up, removing his arm from her shoulder, almost pushing her away. 'You have behaved like a lunatic all night and now you're trying that showbiz medium crap act on me – me, of all people. Stop it, Becky. I have no idea what you're playing at, but I deserve better than that.'

Becky just smiled. 'What?' she said to the thin air by the fireplace. 'Ask him what?' She put her head on one side. 'Hugh, sit down. Your father says he knows that you hide the vodka under the sofa, and he wants to know if you are ever going to tell your mother that you pawned her diamond ring when you were twenty-one and needed cash for that production of Ibsen's *Doll's House*? Will you ever tell your mother, Hugh?'

Now Hugh was really angry. No one, apart from the pawnbroker in Watford, knew about that ring. His mother thought it lost and had claimed on the insurance. Everyone was happy, and his play was produced. He looked at Becky, his hair flopping down and his eyes narrowed. 'What the fuck are you playing at?' he asked slowly.

'I can see your father, Hugh.'

Hugh looked again at the space by the fireplace.

'Something happened to me tonight.' Becky's hand came up to her face and swept away her hair. 'It was dark, and I was very afraid.' She looked at Hugh. 'More afraid than you could ever know.' She looked down. 'But then light came and pushed the dark away. When you and Olly came into the studio, it was as if someone had lifted a veil. I can see.' She laughed. 'All that act we have created, the hand on the arm, the is-there-a-father-figure-just-passed crap… *I can see it*, Hugh. I can actually see it!'

Hugh stared at her. The grey eyes were shining in the firelight. He was the one who had created her act, coached her performance for ten years, and he knew Becky well enough to know when she was acting. This was real. Hugh sat down, his hair falling forward, his eyes constantly flicking to that empty space by the fireplace and then back to Becky.

He did not like this – feeling like a punter. He despised them, the needy, wide-eyed miracle-seekers longing for proof of life on the Other Side. Hugh felt smeared with their desperation. Now he felt vulnerable, amazed, creeped out, unsure what he was hearing and yet unable to dispute that Becky was talking about things no one could know. Hell, stuff even he had forgotten about. Tempus Fugit. Hugh's mind was reeling. He needed a drink, two drinks, it took all of his self-control not to reach out for the vodka bottle hidden under the sofa and to swallow the lot.

The thought of his bigoted, stupid, judgmental father who had rejected him when he'd had the courage to come out... to even think that he was here, in this flat, when he'd been cremated years ago was just a step too far. Hugh had shared Becky's belief that the Other Side and the spiritual, psychic circus were just smoke and mirrors and ripe for exploitation. They had exploited grief and that longing from so many for an answer to the random nature of life that organised religion failed to fill. They had constructed an industry designed to fill the void. Right now though, he felt as though he were in that void. He hated it. There was a ripple of fear, too. And that mutual hatred between father and son was hardly comforting if dear, dead Papa was indeed propping up the mantelpiece, spouting home truths.

Hugh took a deep breath. 'Tell me what you see.'

Becky described his dead father perfectly. By the time she had finished repeating what the spirit was saying, Hugh's anger at Becky was turning into something else. He felt shock at the messages and anger at his dead father. But his feelings towards Becky had changed profoundly.

He realised that he was terrified of her.

Becky fell asleep on his Chesterfield sofa, exhausted after her jaunt of metamorphosing into a full-blown medium. Hugh had fetched a duvet and pillow, carefully avoiding the space where Becky said his dead father had been standing. She assured him that he had gone now and all she wanted was sleep. Hugh didn't sleep. He left all the lights on that night, his business brain churning, his emotions veering from disbelief to fear and back again several times. As he left Becky in the lounge, he looked down at the sleeping redhead, wondering if all the vodka was affecting his grip on reality. His hand swept back the floppy hair, his face drawn. He didn't swig any more vodka from the bottle that night.

Becky had described all of it: the darkness, the smell, the voices, that thrum, thrum, thrum. She had frightened Hugh when she spoke of the shapes pressing into the glass walls and that one voice announcing, 'We are here.' Hugh had watched her as she spoke and he didn't doubt the story.

When Becky spoke of the light – a blessed, total light – she spoke as if salvation had scooped her out of the blackness. Now, his main source of profit claimed that the dead were actually speaking to her. Hugh was in a state of confusion. They'd had a future that seemed certain, built on past success making this hocus pocus up. What if the hocus pocus was now real? Hugh kicked off the silk sheets as he lay in his bed, wondering whether this was just a nightmare starring his dead father, a rocking horse, and a redhead gone stark staring nuts? Sleep did not come.

Becky slept deeply. No darkness came to claim her. Not that night.

The violinist stood in a pool of pure, white light.

Dressed in white tie and tails, his body moved to the sweep of the bow against the strings of the ancient instrument. A triangular light shone down on him from a single point above his head and expanded downwards, bathing him in brightness and obscuring everything else. The illusion was complete – in all the world there was only this man playing the violin, standing suspended as the instrument resonated with the music. That sound: beautiful, melodic, filling the air with melancholy and sadness, yet somehow also such a joyous sound. It was as if he played to touch the soul. Faultlessly, fingers and wrist and arm connected with the instrument as shoulders and back arched into each note. His black hair, swept back from his forehead, was long around the nape of the neck, framing his aquiline features that were focused on the bow, as brain and sinew combined with wood and string to produce a sound of liquid, soaring intensity.

Becky Moran knew that he was not really there. However, it was as though he played just for her. A recital for one. As she looked at the violinist in his shard of light, she realised that he was not flesh and blood but an echo, an imprint, a musician long gone but, in spirit, playing that melancholy piece to show her that his energy and his music still existed. Becky felt no fear; indeed, she welcomed this. The musician was performing a salute to her in his expression of his very being, his talent and life force lingering from somewhere on the Other Side, able to demonstrate what had defined his life. Now he was playing to someone who could see and hear what he once was. The last note held. The violin reverberated and became silent. The musician looked at Becky, took the violin from under his chin, and bowed. The light was extinguished. He was gone.

Becky had at first thought she was asleep. However, she looked into the darkness and still saw the outline on her retina where that triangle of light had been. As it began to fade, she saw the shape of Hugh's living room here in the London flat, the shadow of the curtains, the fireplace, the door to Hugh's bedroom half open. She was fully awake. After the fear and confusion of the last twelve hours, that music had left her feeling hopeful and at peace.

Just a day ago, Becky would have said that what she had just experienced was a vivid dream. Now she realised that she had been given a solo virtuoso performance, not in a dream but in spirit. It was a gesture of kindness and gratitude from a force she could not begin to understand, music sent to soothe her – almost a welcome. Becky Moran knew that life had changed. What she had no concept of was just how, or indeed how much.

Becky looked at the clock above the fireplace in Hugh's flat. It was five in the morning. She knew sleep would not return and got up to go into Hugh's pristine kitchen to make some coffee.

Hugh drove Becky back to Cambridge that morning. They had both woken early and sat sipping coffee, silently contemplating the events of the last few hours. The rain had stopped, at last, but there was a lot of surface water on the roads. They were both quiet as they left London behind. Becky didn't mention the violinist; she thought Hugh would just explode with anger. As he dropped her off at her tiny mews house on Histon Road, he looked at her directly.

'Last night. Was that for real?'

Becky nodded. 'I need some time to think. I was very frightened. But something has changed, Hugh.' She got out of the car, and Hugh accelerated sharply, driving off to his own home in St Neots.

Becky let herself into the mews house. It was tiny, an executive two up, two down with a patch of garden, but it was her base here in the south, near the Divine Diva offices where she and Hugh ran their psychic empire. Becky rented this house but also owned an attic flat in a converted Methodist chapel in Leeds. It was near her parents and she used it as a base to see clients from the north and Scotland.

Becky felt grubby. She showered and changed into a clean white shirt and black skinny jeans with sensible flat brogues, and then walked into Cambridge to get some food. The air was fresh that September morning and she enjoyed the walk. Her Marks and Spencer carrier bag swung on her arm as she unlocked the front door on her return, the bag filled with fresh food and a bottle of wine for her evening meal. She dumped the bag on the worktop in the white galley-style kitchen, took off her jacket and began to unpack. Then she stopped suddenly.

She could distinctly hear the sound of a violin. The same flow of music she'd heard in Hugh's flat in the early hours of the morning was coming softly from upstairs. She raised her head. Somehow, the sound was not so joyful. Becky frowned and drew breath as fear hit her solar plexus. That rotting smell was back, the same as she had inhaled in her radio studio last night. She pressed herself against a kitchen cupboard. That feeling of intense fear was back. She tried to think how to escape the smell, the sound, the fear. All sense of peace and wellbeing was gone.

The sound of the violin was gradually getting louder, discordant now, a slow mockery of the beauty of the performance in the bright light that Becky had watched in the small hours of this morning. The notes were slightly off-key, played out of sequence and building to a screech; and with each strident note, the light was fading.

She could tell that the music was coming from above her, from her bedroom. She knew she had to get out, and fast. Despite her fear, Becky edged herself towards the kitchen door. The back door to the garden was in the living room and she could get out through the French windows. Too far, she calculated, too far. If she could just get out into the hallway she could reach the front door in half a dozen steps. Just one foot, slowly, carefully, in front of the other. She willed her legs to move. In the gloom, she could see the staircase on her right and the door to the living room, closed, to the left. If she reached the front door, the busy street, the traffic, the people, the light and air would all be within reach, a sanctuary away from this sound and whatever was making it.

Becky moved slowly, her eyes straining, darting ahead and flicking to each side of her once-familiar home. The violin solo was now mocking, twisted, not so much a semblance of any tune, more a hacking of bow on string, played in anger and in derision. There was nothing familiar in that music anymore. She had reached the staircase, with the front door two steps away, when the music suddenly stopped.

That stench was thick in the air and now Becky felt again as if the physical world was slipping into that converse reality she had experienced at the Cube.

The hallway, narrow at the best of times, seemed to shrink inwards. As the light receded, the walls were almost straining towards each other. The front door had shrunk too and was far, far away, only to be reached now by a long, narrow, shifting corridor. She could just about see the metal of the key, still in the door where she left it on the inside after locking herself in. Becky knew this was impossible. Her rational brain was trying to keep up with what was happening around her and was failing. The air was heavy with that rank odour – heavy, oppressive, dark. Her hands now looked bleached out – like an old x-ray, the bones visible through her flesh.

Becky shook her head and glanced down, wondering why the very floor beneath her feet had become a deep black pit, over which she was balancing on what felt like a very narrow plank.

Any move and she would tumble down, down into that dark void.

The walls continued to heave inwards. Becky heard her own heartbeat, rapid and strong, and she struggled not to scream. She knew that if she tried to, no sound would come out of her lungs anyway. It was as if her mouth had been sewn shut, like a corpse prepared for the grave by a psychotic mortician who wanted to stitch her body into silence for eternity.

Then, a single note from the violin. It sounded dull, scraped at leisure across the strings. Then again. And again. A thrum, thrum from an instrument hewn in Hell. Then silence.

Becky turned her head to look upstairs.

She saw that there was more than John Dee's other dimension – the fourth – in this newborn world. There was a fifth. A dark shape was gliding down what now appeared to be an impossibly long staircase. This thing, this shape, this being, seemed to shift in texture from solid to soft, from a human shape into a demonic collection of dark shreds flying from where its head should have been in a trailing shroud, streaming remnants of an amorphous body, the eyes darkly gleaming. But it was the mouth, the open maw in that shape-shifting head, which almost made Becky's heart stop. In the second she looked up that gaping hole was glowing red and studded with rows of sharp, white, pointed teeth.

It was bearing down on her, whispering her name, hungry, needy, now descending with speed. Becky knew in her soul that what it wanted, above Heaven and Earth in this parallel reality, quite simply was her.

CHAPTER FOUR

The evil was coming for her.

Becky knew that if it reached her, touched her, fed on her, she would become part of that darkness. She could feel the foul air being pushed ahead of it as the shape came closer and closer; she could hear it calling her and, in her mind, she knew she had to get out, get to the light and to the air to save herself.

In terror and desperation, she remembered the way the violinist had bowed his head to her in the early hours of that morning and the peace that had given her. As she closed her eyes, she also remembered the light which had bathed her in the Cube.

Becky summoned up as much energy as she could from these memories and reached out to the living room door on her left. For a moment she felt panic as the very door seemed to lean away from her. Think of the light, the light… and her hand rested, finally, on the handle, and she pushed, almost falling into the living room. There was light, and she stumbled towards the French windows. Without looking behind, one part of her mind imagined that black shape just reaching out and wrapping her inside its dark, shape-shifting wings and the red, sharp mouth biting into her. She turned the key on the French window and stumbled outside.

She heard a deep, outraged howling from inside the house and blackness filled the French windows, one of them hanging open where she had pushed her way outside. She thought the glass may break as the windows bulged outwards, forced by the blackness – but then, as if a switch had been flicked, everything returned to normal.

Becky was on her knees on a patch of grass and gravel, crouched, adrenalin pumping, ready to flee, to run like an athlete on a starting block. Her red hair was straggled over her face. She could hear the traffic on Histon Road, she saw the afternoon sunlight reflect on those very same French windows, the light bright after the darkness that had absorbed them just a few terrifying seconds ago. Her heartbeat was still rapid, her breathing ragged. She hunkered on the gravel, every muscle tense, waiting to see what may follow her through the half-open French window. There was nothing. She strained her hearing in case that demonic violin began once more or that foul stench would envelop her nostrils. Nothing. Becky pushed herself to her feet. She rubbed her mouth, remembering that inability to speak.

It took her an hour to summon the courage to go back into the house. When she did, she ran in, locked the French windows, grabbed her handbag and ran back out of the front door. She wasn't in the house for sixty seconds. She locked the front door behind her and headed for the safety of a small hotel nearby.

Going back into her bedroom in the mews house – the source of that sound, that inexplicable thing on the stairs – never mind the reality of sleeping there that night, was just not going to happen. Who would believe her? Hugh would look at her with contempt. Sarah wouldn't understand, and Olly? Becky would have welcomed Olly just listening to her story – but he had a girl back in Sunderland, and it was Saturday. He would think she had lost her mind. Becky felt ashamed of what had just happened – mainly because she couldn't explain it to anyone. Better to deal with this alone. A hotel, a neutral space with other people around – even if they were strangers – that would help her feel better, more normal. There were no romantic relationships in her life; her job and its deception to date precluded getting too close to anyone. Becky was self-sufficient. Her team were her family.

As she walked quickly away from the mews house, Becky wondered if she would ever feel normal, never mind sleep, again.

'No,' said Olly Harvey, producer of *Medium Wave*, as he held his mobile slightly away from his ear into which some publisher was babbling about her new author who travelled astral planes with Jesus and a dog called Malachi (a black terrier), and who was prepared to put the astral plane-hopping on hold to get on to Becky Moran's show.

'She can bark like the dog and can give a message from Moses,' the voice said, metallic and booming out of the phone like a hysterical Dalek.

'Not interested,' said Olly. 'No, please don't bother sending the press release. Or the book. Thanks for calling *Medium Wave*.' He pressed the disconnect icon on his phone and sighed. Another wackjob, he thought.

Olly Harvey had been at the offices of Divine Diva, a suite of rooms above a bookmaker on Clifton Road, near the railway station in Cambridge, since nine that Monday morning. He had left the Cube late on Friday night and had spent the weekend at home in Cambridge wondering if Becky was all right – she had seemed so freaked out by that power cut. Since arriving at work that morning, fresh for a new week, he had already booked a crew to film the pilot for the TV show, *The Cambridge Medium*. He knew they would be filming in Lincolnshire and hopefully in York, and they had some willing punters up for being filmed having their readings with Becky. He had a couple of months to do the filming, then three weeks for editing and post-production. It was all looking very good on paper.

Sarah had wafted in just a few minutes after him and given him a big smile. 'What a carry-on that was,' she had said, offering a bag of pastries she had bought on her way into the Divine Diva offices.

Olly took a croissant, smiling at her. 'Thanks, Sarah – good weekend?'

Sarah switched on her computer and chuckled. 'Friday night… no power… Hugh in such a bad mood.' Sarah quite liked Hugh being in a bad mood. She loved working for Becky and Olly but thought Hugh was prone to hissy fits and she liked winding him up. She chuckled some more as she sat down to work.

Olly asked Sarah to rebook John X and the black leather-clad vicar for the radio show since they hadn't made it on air thanks to the power cut on Friday night. He frowned when he thought about Becky's behaviour three nights ago. He had texted her over the weekend to check if she was okay and she had replied she was. The office front door opened and Olly looked up expectantly, hoping it was Becky. Instead, he saw Hugh's raddled, clearly hungover face.

'Heavy weekend?' he asked.

'Fuck off, Olly,' was the genial reply.

Hugh Jolly's eyes were bloodshot after a weekend of vodka and nightmares. His hands, always beautifully manicured, were shaking. Most of Sunday had passed in a clink of clear liquid being poured over ice and now he had a cardboard box in the boot of his Range Rover filled with empties. Hugh was nothing if not fastidious in clearing away the evidence of his addiction at the bottle bank.

Sarah Jones, resplendent in a gargantuan purple poncho that reached her ankles and flapped about her arms (bought in a charity shop dedicated to saving the Alpaca), was wafting a pungent odour that reminded Hugh of wet wool and rotting sheep. This didn't help his alcohol-sodden system. Sarah was typing up briefing notes for *Medium Wave*; she nodded hello to Hugh and carried on typing, her earrings clanking as she checked punter lists for the so-called readings.

Sarah was in her fifties and had been a researcher for various daytime TV chat shows before Hugh Jolly hired her as Becky's PA. She organised Becky and the readings, took the bookings, got some details about the person (not to mention payment up front) and did a bit of digging on the client's background. One-to-ones were popular and the waiting list was long. This gave Sarah enough time to gather material: a look at obituaries online, social media, even have a look round someone's local or social group, which could bring up some detail Becky could use. They used private investigators when they needed to. Sarah made sure Becky had full briefing notes for every client and the system worked well.

Deception could be bought.

Hugh opened the window to get some air in and reduce the smell of 'the mouldy one'. Sarah knew about his nickname for her. She didn't care. She loved her vintage clothing and Hugh was just a Gucci-loving, posh, skinny white boy. She had seen enough of them in her time. Sarah was divorced, and she put all her energy into the job. She liked Becky and working for Divine Diva was better than the grind of daytime TV.

Clutching a large mug of black coffee, in the hope it would steady his hands, Hugh went to stand behind Olly. He peered at his computer screen, looking at the list of guests Olly had lined up for future programmes. There were repeated interview requests from the self-proclaimed healer and unicorn devotee, Bert Brookings. His people were bombarding Olly on a daily basis and, although Olly thought him a total unicorn-peddling flake (Olly snorted every time he said the word 'unicorn'), he was their main advertiser on *Medium Wave*. So Olly had booked him for an interview with Becky on the live radio show later next month. Hugh laughed out loud when he saw that name. 'He's after presenting Becky's show,' Olly told him.

'Yup, and let's hope he brings the unicorn in,' was Hugh's response.

Bert Brookings was based in the Brecon Beacons and ran an international company, all over the Internet, offering cures for cancer by the laying on of hands. There were webinars, YouTube videos, and six-month courses on harnessing the *Power of the Unicorn*. He would have to catch one first, Olly had thought grimly. Bert was big on the speaking circuit, spending much of his time in America where the unicorn and angel community loved him. He spent thousands advertising his Healing Roadshows up and down the UK. He had asked if Divine Diva wanted him for their radio show. Hugh had exploded at that suggestion.

'Anyone peddling unicorn healing needs a bloody shrink – the charlatan – I am more likely to employ a dead slug dressed in tinsel than that Welsh idiot!'

So, Bert was still waiting.

The rest of the guest list on Olly's computer screen was the usual collection of reincarnated royalty, chakra balancers, and ghost hunters. One name caught Hugh's eye – an antique collector from York who said he had an antique mirror which was cursed.

'Who's that?' asked Hugh, pointing to the name.

'Max Smythe? Interesting one, that. I'm thinking it will make for the TV pilot. This man claims he has an antique mirror with a history going back to World War Two and it's brought misery to everyone who has ever owned it. He says there's a documented provenance.'

'Why doesn't he just chuck it down the tip?'

'He has. It keeps coming back,' Olly told him.

'Oh, give over. You've been doing this job too long.' Hugh turned away and went to pour some more coffee.

Olly said nothing. This story intrigued him more than most. He was going to call Max Smythe if he had time before the production meeting and would brief Becky later. He was planning to pitch this antique mirror story for the TV pilot and was going up to York – he would take Becky with him – to see what it was really all about.

Olly saw he had a missed call from Brookings on his iPhone. He ignored it, checked for other messages, put his headphones on, and began to digitally edit the opening sequence for next Friday night's show. On his desk was a box. Someone had sent him a clear plastic replica of a crystal skull, with a note promising to bring the real thing in on Friday. The dome of the skull, which was unusually large and just emerging from the bubble wrap, gleamed under the fluorescent lights of the office. Olly thought it may make a good doorstop.

The online team were tucked away in their own office with the door shut as usual. Computer geeks liked privacy, mainly because much of their day was spent online gaming and work got in the way. Hugh knew this, but he also knew that they got the blog, ticket sales for the big theatre venues, and the daily supernatural updates done, so he cut them some slack. He could put up with geeks if they turned a big profit. They had printed out the ticket sales for Becky's next theatre show at the Dominion in a couple of weeks' time and left it on Hugh's desk. Hugh had been pleased to see they had gone up over the weekend. The fact that *Medium Wave* had been taken off the air by a lightning strike made four lines in the *Evening Standard* and a quarter-page in the *Daily Mail* on Saturday morning, with an archbishop implying that it was retribution from God for peddling the supernatural. There was a picture of Becky Moran smouldering in black and white alongside the copy.

Hugh seemed pleased. Getting Becky Moran into the papers, without anyone actually doing an exposé on what they did, was a lucky escape.

Olly glanced at his watch, took his headphones off, and decided he did have time to make that call about the mirror. He was curious. He picked up his phone and dialled.

In the ancient city of York, antique dealer Max Smythe was sitting at his eighteenth-century writing desk at the rear of his shop, talking to Olly Harvey on the house phone. As he talked to Olly, Max's eyes rested on what had become known as the Mirror, on display at the front of the shop with the ornate blackened frame softly reflecting the light, the glass brightly polished and reflecting the contents of his shop. Max watched the Mirror constantly.

Olly had called to arrange a trip to York with Becky Moran for later that week. Max looked down at his diary. 'Yes, Wednesday would be good,' he said. 'Can you both get here for about eleven thirty?'

Max came from a long line of antique dealers. Now in his early seventies, he chose to dress in a simple black suit and wear a tie every day. He had white hair, immaculately combed, and all his own teeth. The business had been passed down from his father, Louis. The family were German Jews who had got out of Munich when Hitler began his rise to power. Max's father had come to Yorkshire and had managed to import many treasures.

Some members of the family had then taken the steamer to America but York suited Max perfectly. He loved this city, where he had been born and brought up after the war. The shop was in Swinegate, and a steady stream of well-heeled tourists and even better-heeled locals passed through the door with the tinkling bell. Fine art, antique furniture, enough trinkets to satisfy those who liked Venetian glass and Victorian art, and some major pieces of Art Deco furniture ensured that Max had carried on the family tradition well. His sons would carry on with the business when he chose to retire.

But now, Max was frightened.

Out of desperation, he had contacted Becky Moran at The Voice of Britain, the radio station he had playing softly in his shop every day, because of this object he had acquired from Poland. It seemed that no one, not even his rabbi, would believe what had happened since the antique mirror had arrived in a consignment from Krakow.

Max imported many objects. He had good international connections and Europe was an excellent source of antiques. A contact in Poland had been commissioned to oversee a house clearance from a grand apartment building in the centre of Krakow, dilapidated and belonging to a family who had reached the end of the line. Max had looked at the catalogue online and selected pieces he knew his customers would buy. His agent paid the bill, took his commission and arranged the transport.

Among the lot was this large, gothic-style mirror, though Max had no memory of the object being in the catalogue. The glass was clear with just a light patina of age. A metre and a half long and a metre wide, the frame was ebony, with ornate scrollwork extending to a point at both the top and bottom. At each outer edge was a carved black rose. The detail was exquisite. The back of the mirror was a solid, thin sheet of ebony. Max was puzzled to find it in the carefully packed shipment from Poland, but he knew he would find a buyer for it quickly. The mirror was a thing of beauty. He planned to ask four thousand for it and knew he would get it.

In the manifest was a letter from his Polish agent along with a faded envelope, found attached to the back of the mirror, which had been removed for shipping to the UK. Max had put the two envelopes to one side to examine later as he prepared the collection from Poland for display in the shop.

It wasn't until two weeks later that he opened both of the envelopes with a growing sense of fear, which had begun when visiting tourists had seen the Mirror the day he put it on display. He had hung it by the main entrance to the shop where it reflected the daylight and drew the eye on an uncluttered wall. The American and his wife, forty-somethings, both dressed in the ubiquitous Burberry, pounced on it and declared it 'just darling'. The wife especially loved it. She ran her fingers over the ornately scrolled fretwork. 'This would look amazing in your study.' She was smiling at her husband, who stood beside her, their reflection encased by the ebony frame. Their eyes shone in appreciation, a couple from the New World, their image captured in a mirror from the old.

'I could hang it over the desk.' The husband was clearly already picturing it on his wall as he looked at the reflection of them both in that aged glass.

Max had explained that it was an antique from Poland. 'Yes,' he said, 'we can certainly export to Maryland. No problem at all. Why don't I draw up the export costs and documents – go have lunch – I will have everything ready for this afternoon.' The price was agreed, a handshake, Max smiled, and the couple were entranced. As they left his shop and crossed the road, a car flew down Swinegate and hit the wife, flinging her body into the air. The car came out of nowhere. The American woman died on the pavement with her husband sobbing beside her. The ambulance was too late to save her, and Max was in tears, watching the husband crying on the road outside his shop. A terrible day.

Max hadn't made any connection to the Mirror until his cleaner came to him the day after the accident and said she wouldn't go near that thing again. Max looked at her in surprise.

'I saw something,' she said.

'Don't be ridiculous, it was your own reflection.' Max had raised his arms in surprise. The cleaner, Sylvia, a devout Roman Catholic, had crossed herself.

'Mr Smythe, there was a handprint on the glass. I rubbed at it with my cloth and glass cleaner but it just wouldn't move. To be honest, it looked as if it was inside the glass. It was really bloody odd, I can tell you. So I cleaned the frame with my feather duster and turned to do that dining table…' she had pointed to the six-seater in dark oak he had bought in Crewe at a house clearance, '… and when I turned back to have another go at the glass, the handprint had gone and I saw something move – inside the glass. It was like it was looking at me. Then, I swear to God, the glass went black.'

Max had glanced over at the Mirror, hanging on display at the front of the shop, the glass unblemished and shining in the light, just one object among so many.

'Look at it – nothing wrong with it, Sylvia,' he said.

'Exactly, Mr Smythe. But I know it went black and you can't tell me it didn't.'

Sylvia said she would never go near the thing again.

Then a flood had ruined some stock he kept in the cellar. Someone had smashed the front window of the shop shortly after the Mirror arrived; the insurance covered it, but now he'd had to install a metal grill. Bad luck seemed to haunt him. His doctor had warned him that his heart needed a stent and he should avoid stress.

But now there were the recurring dreams of an old, evil-looking woman who appeared at the foot of his bed, pointing at him and mouthing words he could not hear or understand. She was dressed in black, her hair wild, her face twisted with the flesh hanging from her jowls, the eyes black and gleaming. Every night the same dream. Every night he would awake frightened and with his heart racing. Not a superstitious man, he couldn't help wondering whether the Mirror may somehow be connected to all these things.

It was after he opened the two letters from Poland that had come with the consignment that he took the thing down from the wall and threw it into the skip outside at the back of the shop. The next morning it was back, undamaged, sitting inside the shop, propped near the door. Max knew that was impossible as all the doors had been locked. He had then wrapped the Mirror in a blanket and told his son, Fabien, to take it to the local tip.

Fabien was shocked. 'But Dad, it's worth something – we never throw antiques away!' Max had been adamant, and Fabien shrugged his shoulders, probably wondering if his father wasn't getting too old for this trade.

Fabien assured Max he had thrown it down into the large hopper and heard it fall, the ancient glass shattering on the other rubbish. Max hadn't explained why he wanted to be rid of a potentially valuable antique, but he was now confident that whatever it was had gone.

Next morning, the Mirror had been leaning at the side of his eighteenth-century writing desk, intact, waiting for him. Fabien called to say he had been awake all night after a very bad dream in which some old woman in black was shouting at him. Max felt his heart flutter wildly. After talking to Rabbi Mayen, he had picked up the phone to Voice of Britain to talk to that radio show *Medium Wave*.

Rabbi Mayen, after a lot of persuasion, had said he thought there was a remote possibility – 'but clearly nonsense' – that this could be a malicious spirit. The rabbi went silent on the phone as Max told the story. 'It has been known that an object can be haunted – or even possess the living. But Max, this is the twenty-first century and you are an educated man of reason.' The rabbi seemed concerned that his old friend could be succumbing to age or maybe even the onset of dementia.

'Humour me,' said Max, quietly and calmly. 'What do you know of these spirits?'

Rabbi Mayen sighed. 'Not much. I have heard they choose their owner – which is you.' As Max now owned the Mirror (as the letters from Poland had explained) it was now his unless he could sell it to someone else. Rabbi Mayen had then asked Max, 'Are you overworking, my friend? Time to retire?'

'No, but thank you, Rabbi, for your time.' The rabbi said he would come and see him very soon and suggested he get some rest.

Max had agreed and, as he put the phone down, he was looking at the ornate frame of the cursed object propped by his desk. But he knew from one of those letters that if the Mirror didn't want a new owner, then nothing could make it move. Max had reluctantly put it back on the wall, hoping someone would buy it and take whatever was attached to it away. No one had. He now avoided looking at it directly as he straightened the frame or went anywhere near the thing. He told himself it was just his imagination when he inadvertently saw something move in the glass.

Max could tell that Olly was intrigued by his story. He and Becky would be with Max late Wednesday morning. 'We just want to have a look at the mirror, let Becky see it – and then if we are in agreement, we can bring a film crew up at a later date.'

'Thank you, Mr Smythe, I look forward to meeting you.'

'I look forward to meeting you both. Goodbye.' As Max replaced the receiver on the telephone, he couldn't help looking up across the shop.

The Mirror's glass was completely black.

CHAPTER FIVE

The main office door at Divine Diva opened and Becky smiled as she stepped in.

'Good morning,' she said. Hugh was instantly jealous. She looked refreshed and her face was flushed as if she had just taken a brisk walk. It was a cool but sunny Monday morning and her red hair was ruffled from the walk. She looked slim, healthy and young as she took off her jacket. Simply dressed in a white t-shirt and skinny black jeans, the trademark Louboutins discarded for flat boots, the off-duty Becky looked fresh and clean. Hugh had been imagining that her weekend had been as difficult as his own, twisted with scenes from Friday night, writhing with more delusions of the dead appearing, and worrying about one's mental health. Clearly not.

'You are late,' he snarled at Becky.

Becky Moran just smiled. She sat down on the red sofa in the soft-seating area where they had their meetings. 'Here now.'

Sarah brought her a coffee over. 'Good weekend?'

Becky nodded but didn't look Sarah in the eye; in fact, Hugh noticed she wasn't looking anyone in the eye. He thought she looked distracted.

'Great. What a night on Friday, Becky. You should have seen them in the Green Room – the vicar was praying. Were you okay? Do you want a croissant?'

'No, thanks.' Becky smiled again. Sarah nodded and took a seat next to her as they waited for Olly and Hugh to join them on the soft seats.

'I have something to say,' Becky announced, looking at Hugh.

Hugh rolled his eyes and his hand swept back the floppy fringe. 'Becky, stop with the "I see dead people" act, will you? We have a lot of work to do and—'

Becky stood up. 'Sorry, Hugh, but Olly and Sarah need to know.' Hugh gestured at her to shut her mouth, but Becky didn't look at him.

'Something happened on Friday night at the Cube.'

Sarah looked puzzled. 'I know, it was a power cut and we went off air and we've rebooked the guests.'

Olly looked at Becky, instantly curious, remembering her strange behaviour. 'What?' he asked.

Becky sat down again.

'I don't know what. What I do know is that something happened and…' She swallowed. 'I am not sure how, but since Friday I have seen spirit people, including Hugh's dead father, and now I can see others. I can actually see them. This is not an act anymore.'

Olly laughed. Sarah frowned. Hugh put his head in his hands.

'I'm serious,' Becky said. She sipped her coffee.

She spoke for a quarter of an hour with no interruption. She told them about the smells, the voices and the darkness, the bright light, and then seeing Hugh's father at the flat in Green Park. She described a violinist she had seen in Hugh's flat early on Saturday morning (Hugh's jaw dropped; he was annoyed), and her feeling of peace and acceptance. Her voice didn't falter. She spoke clearly and, apart from a tremble of fear when she talked about what happened in the studio just after the lights went out, her conviction was clear. Then she turned and looked at Sarah.

'Your brother, your twin, is with you, Sarah. He was standing next to you when I came in. He looks so much like you and he is laughing. He is saying you are amazing. He wants to thank you for not forgetting him and says his passing, well, it was an accident, wasn't it?'

Sarah nodded, looking shocked at what she was hearing; there were tears in her eyes. 'It wasn't anyone's fault. He shouldn't have been playing by the river bank. He fell in.' Sarah was weeping now. Sarah looked up at Hugh and Olly, her face grief-stricken. 'When we were ten, my twin brother drowned. He was playing on his own, without me.' Sarah put her hand over her face and spoke quietly, crying. 'They didn't find his body for a week, he washed up six miles downstream. I always feel a part of me is missing.' Sarah's hands twisted on her lap, clenching very tight. 'I miss him every day. I know my parents kept the horror of it from me when I was a child, but I know what they went through. What I am still going through.' Sarah raised her head and looked at Becky in wonder, tears running down her face. 'Does he know how much we love him?'

'He knows, he loves you, he is telling me he misses you, but he is fine.' Sarah bent over, her head down. Becky held her and reassured her that everything was okay.

Olly watched, his eyebrows getting higher and higher. Becky turned to speak to him, but he stood up.

'No!' said Olly. 'Look, Becky, I have no idea what's happening here. Hugh looks like death, Sarah is upset, but you can cut that hocus pocus rubbish with me.' Becky opened her mouth, but Olly continued. 'Let's be clear. You can say what you think you see all you want, but you don't do it with me. I don't believe any of it. All I want is to do my job and do it well. Never run that act by me, Becky. I mean it.'

Olly turned on his heel. 'I'm going for a walk. When I get back, I don't want to speak of this again.' He picked up his jacket and quietly closed the main office door behind him.

Hugh looked at Becky, who was now anxiously biting her lip, with her arm around a sobbing Sarah, and he wondered if Olly would ever come back. He sighed. It was nearly eleven on a Monday morning and Hugh felt as though his whole world was tipping on its axis.

The weekend had not been easy for Becky Moran at all. After what she had gone through – survived – at the mews house, she had checked into the hotel. She had undressed and stood in a hot shower for twenty minutes, trying to cleanse herself of the events of the last few hours. She put her head under the hot burst of water and wondered if she were going mad. She sincerely hoped not.

But when she remembered the darkness she had tensed in fear and waited to inhale that rotting smell again. The light, however, she had felt uplifted by. She'd sat on Hugh's Chesterfield absolutely terrified by the man standing by the fireplace. She knew Hugh's father wasn't there in any physical sense and had tried to shut out the fact that he was talking to her, saying some shocking things about Hugh. In the end, she had acknowledged this entity and told Hugh what was there and what was being said. Somehow, his reaction made it real.

She saw the dead.

They could speak, after all. The terror of what happened in her radio studio and then in her mews house in Cambridge made her shudder.

Becky knew something had emerged, live on air when she touched John Dee's crystal. Whatever that bauble had been used for, that strange power had found her and opened a door to something dark, put her in its path. Becky knew the darkness wanted her. She also knew there was a balance – a light – something pure that was trying to stave off the blackness. Becky was ashamed. She had peddled these so-called supernatural powers as authentic for so long; they now felt very real indeed. Her fear of her perceived new world was overwhelming. She felt hunted.

In her hotel room that Saturday night, Becky sat on the bed with every light switched on. The shock of what had happened hit her hard. She trembled. She left the curtains open; it was now dark on that September evening and she took comfort in seeing the traffic move through Cambridge, the cyclists with their flashing rear lights, the sounds and sights of a university town winding down after another academic day. She put the TV on to extinguish the silence and felt very alone. There was no one she could confide in – even Hugh thought she had gone mad.

Becky did not believe in God. She had no defined faith. After all, she had spent the last decade ridiculing organised belief, feeding into an industry that exploited the alternative, an industry that pandered to those in search of something paranormal to ease the mundane.

She had met many who thought an enlightened spiritual life meant believing in guardian angels. She had met astral travellers. She had shared platforms with so-called psychics who blinded their believers with predictions; she saw the rune readers, Tarot card readers, even those who did complicated things with the I Ching to clarify the future.

There were the ancient astronaut theorists who believed the pyramids of Egypt and the stone spheres of Costa Rica were evidence of extraterrestrial tinkering in man's development, with an energy somehow linked to the solar system. Look hard enough, they said, and even the ancient Egyptians had engravings of light bulbs. These gurus led tours for the gullible in light aircraft and flew over the Nazca Lines in Southern Peru to gawp at the geoglyphs etched in the soil, proclaiming them as alien handicraft calling cards and conclusive proof that they'd been here. It would be hinted that they had never left.

There were the conspiracy theorists too, who claimed that governments were keeping us in the dark like mushrooms. (Becky struggled with the idea that any government could keep a secret in this age of social media and smartphones and wondered why aliens, their abductees and UFOs were not outed every day.) The new temple of the absurd was on YouTube with a video to help reinforce whatever belief one chose. A few minutes on there and you could even see images of the Black Knight satellite, ten tonnes of space hardware orbiting the Earth and thirteen thousand years old, its origins unknown. Naturally, the Pentagon regularly issued statements saying that its existence was a fantasy, and the conspiracy theorists loved that.

Ghost hunters: how she had laughed at them, walking around old buildings with bits of electrical equipment trailing wires behind them as they searched for cold spots and waited for floorboards to creak, leading anorak-clad groups who carried Ouija boards in the hope of a three-raps-for-yes.

The whole spooky circus existed to replace what an altar and priest had once provided: a belief in something higher, an order and a faith to keep us in line.

Becky began to laugh now, wondering what ghost hunters would have made of what had happened to her these last few hours. Her laughter subsided as she shook out her hair and looked at herself in the mirror over the standard desk found in every hotel room. She knew that if she opened the drawer a Gideon Bible would be sitting there. How ironic. Her reflection was pale and those grey eyes looked tired. She remembered reading an American study that concluded the brain was hardwired to believe in some higher power, a creator, and that from prehistoric times to the modern day, faith was just a matter of neurological wiring. That made complete sense to Becky; it was as significant as Crick and Watson working out the structure of DNA here in Cambridge.

However, she was not just part of that paranormal circus, with her radio show, website, theatre shows, and a TV series in the offing; now she could actually see this paranormal dimension. Becky didn't know if she was being punished for years of deception, with some dark force that wanted her very soul now focused on her, or if she had been given a gift – a gift to see into another dimension.

She knew now, for certain, that it was real, that people didn't just evaporate when they died and that somehow spirit survived and envied the living. She knew that love went on even when a person passed over. Becky also knew that it wasn't just the good who survived. Whatever was waiting on the Other Side could be evil.

And something had its eye on her. Becky shuddered. She had seen something unspeakable, something inexplicable bearing down on her, speaking her name, coming for her. She was terrified. She looked around the hotel room, checking the darker corners, and she even opened the wardrobe door to see if there was anything hiding. She took a drink of the wine she'd bought on the way as she sat on the edge of the bed in the brightly lit, ubiquitously styled hotel room.

Whilst her lack of belief in God had not altered, Becky Moran's view of how the universe was structured and of our very existence, was radically changed. She felt as though her compass was lost and that navigating her way ahead was going to be almost impossible.

As she walked from the hotel to the Divine Diva offices on Monday morning – she still didn't feel she could stay in the mews house, although she had quickly retrieved some clothes and a bag in broad daylight, keeping the front door wide open as an escape route – Becky felt as if she were newborn in a world that had been hidden from

her for thirty-three years.

She existed, as before, in three dimensions. Her reflection in the mirror was the same. However, she now saw another dimension, a fifth layer of existence. It was as if a heavy veil had been lifted. She could see what others could not: existing alongside those walking the bustling streets of Cambridge were figures, more like energies, walking close to pedestrians or standing alone on street corners. She heard their voices as she walked past them.

One of them realised that Becky could sense he was there. She saw his energy as he moved beside her; she distinctly heard a man's voice asking, 'Where am I? Do you know? I just want to go back... I am lost.'

Becky put her head down and kept on walking. The voice faded. It was as though she was now attracting the spirits. They could feel she was there and they came to her. She could hear them clearly and see their energy. Some brought more than one family member to show her that they were all together. It was becoming a cacophony of energy and voices and Becky had been astonished by it.

Later that Monday afternoon, after his outburst, Olly had asked to see Becky when he came back to the office after a couple of hours. They'd gone to a coffee shop near the station. As they stirred their cappuccinos, Olly had reiterated that he didn't want any part in – and didn't accept – Becky's new abilities.

'Sorry, Becky, I just want to do the job in hand.'

Becky had not been able to look at Olly: the one person she thought may listen, may even understand her and offer some support, was rejecting this surreal experience out of hand.

'Of course, Olly, I don't want to upset you. I just don't see why you are so upset? You seem far more uncomfortable with what I'm saying now, after what happened to me on Friday night and since than when deceiving everyone was the norm, not three days ago?'

Olly blushed. 'I don't know. But I'm not falling for any supernatural claptrap. It's entertainment, Becky. I'm a producer. That's it.'

He stared hard out of the café window, his honest face full of tension.

They agreed to an uneasy truce.

Back at Divine Diva, Sarah wanted to talk. She was still crying but seemed anxious to tell Becky more about her twin. 'I always lived as though a part of me was lost,' Sarah said, wiping her eyes. 'I was first in my family to get a degree, something our extended family in Jamaica are very proud of. I did it for him, I did it for us. We never talk about what happened – it's just too painful.' She looked at Becky with such sadness, it was hard to hold her gaze. Becky gently explained to Sarah that her brother had gone now. Sarah thanked her warmly, a plaintive reminder of all the punters Becky had fooled and who had received comfort from her so-called readings. Becky realised that, whatever this was, she now had a responsibility.

Producer and presenter sat down to go through the programme for this week, along with the details of the two punters who had 'called in' to the show for the 'readings' Becky would do. All the research was done so Becky would be right on the money with her chat about the Other Side. Becky felt sure she wouldn't need any of the research set up for the punters anymore. It was a sobering thought. Olly was matter of fact. He confirmed their road trip to York in two days' time, handing her a briefing note on Max Smythe and the Mirror. Becky thanked him.

'This could make a great TV pilot,' he said. 'Even if it is wackjob nonsense.'

Becky was sad to see Olly turn away from her, return to his computer, and put his headphones on as he continued to edit the opening sequence for Friday's edition of *Medium Wave*.

The day ended with Hugh needing an assurance from Becky that they were on course as planned.

'More so,' answered Becky, with a certainty she didn't feel. Hugh shook his head and said they had better be.

CHAPTER SIX

On Wednesday morning, Becky Moran was waiting at King's Cross station near the line of excited tourists dressed in scarves and Harry Potter specs, waiting to be photographed at Platform 9¾ before catching their real trains to real places from the real platforms. She stood under the latticed, arching roof and waited for Olly. Dressed in the trademark black dress, Louboutin shoes, and a simple jacket from Zara, she was warm in the September air. She had caught the express train up from Cambridge, leaving at 7 a.m. because Olly had said he would meet her at King's Cross for their train to York; he would be in London the night before after a production meeting at the Cube.

The past four nights had been spent at the small hotel in Cambridge. She had gone back to the mews house the day before during daylight, leaving the front door wide open again and climbing the very normal-looking staircase before taking a deep breath and going into her bedroom. She'd collected her clothes, make-up, computer and charger, rapidly looking around and ready to run if the light faded or that terrible smell came back. There was nothing. She'd run back downstairs, bag in hand, taken a deep breath, grabbed the bag of fresh food she'd left on the kitchen counter on Saturday, binned it, run out of the front door and locked it behind her.

She had slept for four nights with every light blazing in that hotel room, her perception of spirit energy now very sharp. On the train up to London from Cambridge, there had been energies, clearly taking the route to work as they had in life. She had been spoken to by a female spirit, a bright energy whom Becky saw as a middle-aged woman with soft brown hair, carrying a large handbag. The spirit stood in front of her on the train and spoke as if she were as real as the living on their daily commute to London.

'Will you tell Elsie I am fine? And to get the plumber round to fix the leaking pipe in the roof, or the ceiling will fall in?' The request was conversational.

Becky had no idea who Elsie was and she had learned that if she didn't react, the energy would just fade away. She would imagine an off switch and it seemed to make them disappear. The woman with the handbag stepped away, still speaking, but she dissolved into the ether. Once you adjusted to it, Becky was learning it was quite easy to control. But she shuddered when she thought of that dark entity in her house. She had no idea if an off switch or anything else could make that go away.

On the other hand, Becky knew that if she asked those energies to come to her, they would. Then, she thought, it would get very interesting indeed.

Olly appeared in front of her, kissed her hello on the cheek, and they headed off to the Grand Central train for York. Olly was a bit shamefaced after his outburst at Divine Diva's offices on Monday. He'd had a good production meeting at the Cube, with a request from the Station Controller at Voice of Britain (an Irishman called Aiden O'Conner who liked wearing bow ties and had a gargantuan stomach) to get more supernatural guests in ('More weirdos, Olly, and the weirder the better,' were his actual words). Olly had agreed. God knew, there were enough out there.

Becky was relieved Olly was behaving normally with her. She had been concerned that he may make fun of what she had told him, or shut down their friendship, maybe even their professional relationship. There was no sign of that and, as the train pulled out of King's Cross and headed north, Becky began to relax. On the journey, they looked at the guest list for the coming show this Friday, which included the owner of the crystal skull – the real one – who had sent the plastic copy to Olly and would bring the original to the Cube. Then Olly ran through what he knew about Max Smythe's cursed mirror.

'We can get some great shots of York, you walking through The Shambles by the Minster. I just want to check it all out before we film.'

Becky nodded, knowing he was hopeful they would get a series commissioned.

'What is this mirror, then?' she asked.

'Not a bloody clue,' answered Olly. 'But Smythe doesn't sound like a wackjob.'

They caught a cab from York station and it pulled up outside the antique shop on Swinegate nearly three hours after they'd left London. The area was filled with expensive restaurants, upscale interior furnishing shops, and second-hand bookstores. They got out of the cab and Olly paid the driver. They stood on the pavement and looked at the double windows, filled with good pieces of furniture and Art Deco jewellery. The effect was expensive and welcoming. Olly went through the latched door, holding it open for Becky to walk through. As she did so, her eye caught the ornate ebony mirror hanging on a wall near the door with its glass surface reflecting the daylight.

'Is that it?' she asked.

Max Smythe, immaculate in his black suit, appeared in front of Becky. He took her hand and shook it.

'Miss Moran, welcome.' He looked at the Mirror and quickly looked away again. 'Yes, that's it. Please, come in. You must be Olly. Welcome, welcome...' He quickly ushered them both away to the rear of the shop and indicated they should sit in front of his antique desk. He served coffee from a bone china pot in cups so fine they were almost transparent. They made small talk about train journeys from London, and Max Smythe seemed a little star-struck with the beautiful redhead in his shop, whose voice he knew so well from listening on Friday nights to *Medium Wave*.

Olly got out his notes. He explained that the reason for their visit today was to have a look at the mirror, to hear Max's story, and to learn more about the provenance and the alleged events since the Mirror arrived from Poland, with a view to making a story for their TV pilot. Becky noticed that whilst Max Smythe was over seventy, well dressed and beautifully mannered, there was a tension in his eyes. He looked afraid. If Olly had been more observant, perhaps he may have seen it too. Becky sensed no spirits around Smythe but she was feeling anxious, though she just couldn't source it until she realised that the feeling had started when she'd seen the Mirror.

Max Smythe sat back in his chair. He drew his hands up so that the tips of his fingers were pressed together, arched in front of his face and touching his nose. It almost looked as if he were praying. His white hair was swept back away from his face.

'That thing is cursed. I want to sell it but it will only allow itself to be sold when it chooses a person to buy it. I am the one it's currently chosen.'

Olly's eyebrows rose. Becky said nothing.

In his low voice, his eyes occasionally flicking towards the wall, he told them the story of the sale of contents from an old apartment building in Krakow. He spoke of a trusted agent, a fine collection of items, the instructions to buy what he had selected at the auction – and the fact that he had never chosen the Mirror, that it had never been in the auction catalogue nor on any manifest. It was listed in the export documents, though, as a two-thousand-euros sale. No previous sales records had this item listed. Nevertheless, it had arrived in the Polish consignment with two letters.

He told the story of the accident outside on Swinegate after the Americans had wanted to buy it and of the sad death of the wife. Max was visibly distressed, such a lovely couple, so happy, a terrible accident. The driver was drunk by all accounts. He told them about Sylvia, his cleaner who had been with him for twenty years, who had said she would not return to work while the Mirror was here. No, he didn't know if she would talk to Becky about it. He would ask.

He spoke slowly, quietly, when he described the two attempts to get rid of the object and the fact that it just reappeared in his shop. He paused after describing this, almost as if he thought these two young people in front of him may mock him. They did not. Max then described the dreams that he, his son Fabien, and Sylvia were having, all the dreams the same. They were nightmares. And as he spoke of the old hag, screaming at the foot of his bed, Becky felt cold fear knot in her stomach. She turned her head, looking over her shoulder.

'It turns black,' said Max, nodding towards the wall. Becky looked back at him. Max spoke of the handprints that appeared on the Mirror's surface from time to time, some of them very small like those of a child. Olly stood up and walked back towards the entrance of the shop. There were no customers that lunchtime. 'Don't touch it!' warned Max, half rising out of his seat.

'No way,' muttered Olly.

Max looked at Becky. 'Miss Moran, I know you understand these things.' He gestured to Becky, almost in appeal. 'I'm just at a loss to know what that thing is.'

Less than a week ago, Becky would have derided this story, mentally mocked this quiet, gentle man and given some patter about haunted objects being simply the symptom of an overactive imagination. Now, Becky had no reason not to believe the story being played out in Swinegate in York.

'What did the letters say?' she asked as Olly came and sat down again in the chair next to her.

Max put his glasses on and reached into a drawer of the antique desk. There were two letters, one marked as being from the Polish agent with his letterhead in gold and black. That letter explained that this item had turned up in the consignment and that the agent was investigating where it had come from. The other letter was ancient, on a yellowed sheet of parchment, just a few lines handwritten in Polish in faded black copperplate. It was creased as if it had spent years inside the envelope. The envelope was unmarked. Max explained that it had originally been tucked in between the frame and the smooth ebony back of the Mirror. The agent had removed it for shipping.

Max had a translation of this older letter that he had asked his rabbi to arrange. He told Becky that Rabbi Moyen still had not been to see him in person and was not answering his calls since he had emailed the translation to him.

Max peered over the top of his spectacles. 'You must understand, I have worked with my agent in Poland for years. I trust him. In this,' he held up the letter with the gold and black letterhead, 'he explains to me that the Mirror was in the consignment he collected for delivery to me here in York. He could not find it on the manifest, either, so he assumed it was a mistake. But the auction house said they knew nothing of it. He tried to speak to the estate selling the apartment's contents, but they never responded. My agent decided to export it anyway since it was quite a small object and his letter confirms that the export was legal. He said that if anyone in Krakow wanted it, he knew where it was and would sort it out. He enclosed the other envelope,' Max pointed at the parchment, 'saying that he'd removed it from the back. I didn't read either letter until after the first time the Mirror came back when I tried to get rid of it.'

'Has no one claimed this mirror from Poland?' asked Olly.

'No,' said Max.

Becky was listening intently. 'Mr Smythe, what does that letter, the original old one, actually say?'

Max Smythe went pale. 'Miss Moran, I am trusting you to believe me. I wanted to meet you, never mind the radio show or what you want to film. You may know what I have to do. Will you promise me something?'

Becky leaned forward. 'If I can, Mr Smythe.'

'Just help me be rid of that thing.' He pointed towards it. 'I am begging you, help me, Becky.'

Max Smythe put his hands over his face and began to cry.

Olly was embarrassed to see this lovely, gentle old man sobbing in front of them both. He also felt guilty, because Max Smythe clearly believed that Becky had some sort of gift to help him rid himself of whatever supernatural crap he thought was emanating from the old Polish mirror.

Becky, however, had put her arm over the desk and was making soothing noises to Max. Olly always knew that Becky was damn good at the fakery, but he wondered whether she might be going too far here. For all they knew, Max Smythe could be a wackjob with early onset dementia who liked reading ghost stories at midnight. Olly cleared his throat and Becky sat back in her chair while Max composed himself and took a handkerchief from his top pocket to wipe his eyes.

'I apologise.'

'Tell us,' said Becky. Max glanced over at the Mirror again, then began to tell his story.

'My agent tells me... I will get to this,' he pointed to the parchment again, 'in a moment... Well, I asked him to tell me about the place the antiques came from, the background to the apartment. The estate selling off the contents, they told him it was located in the central square in the city of Krakow. Very old, very grand. The last occupant was a spinster whose family moved into the flat after the war. The family bought it cheaply as the original Jewish family had vanished. You are both aware, I expect, that Auschwitz is about an hour away from Krakow?' Olly and Becky nodded.

'During the war, the Nazis commandeered the apartment. It was occupied by a Nazi sympathiser – a Pole the Germans looked favourably on. Naturally, he wasn't a Jew. So many homes were just taken from their owners. Art was looted. It was chaos and so much was lost. The apartment was often visited by the Nazi military, enjoying Krakow during the war. It is said that, when the wind blew a certain way and the ashes from the death camp fell on the city like snowflakes, the Nazis used to cheer.' Max's eyes filled with tears again. 'Many of our family died in Birkenau, in those gas chambers.'

He pulled himself up in his chair. 'The rumour was that some of the Nazi visitors were obsessed with the occult. It came from Heinrich Himmler, the leader of the SS, who was convinced that ancient artefacts had dark powers and they would ensure the Third Reich lasted forever. It is hearsay, but some rituals were practised in that apartment and that mirror –' he gestured with his head, '– could have been brought to the apartment by one of Himmler's acolytes. Or it might always have been there. It could be French, as far as we know. But I have no idea if it was in Krakow before the occupation, or why the Russians didn't take it when they liberated that part of Poland. Provenance to that degree is lost in war. And communism.'

Max took a sip of coffee. 'What is interesting is that no one knows anything about the mirror. My agent can't clarify if that is actually where it came from or not. Because it was with the consignment from the apartment, we have to assume it came from there. There are no reports or rumours about the family who bought the apartment after the war. They lived there until the old lady died three months ago, in her seventies. That is all we know.

'This letter, which he tells me was stuck on the back of the Mirror, is a warning.' Max picked up a printout of the translation Rabbi Moyen had emailed. 'Please do not read it out loud.' He handed the email to Becky. She looked down and what she read made her blink in astonishment. There was a line from the rabbi at the top of the email, saying that this below was nonsense but here it was, translated by a Polish academic at York University.

> *Beware, casual onlooker, of what you see.*
> *For what you may see is me.*
> *What lies beneath the aged glass*
> *lies trapped, watchful, and reflects your world from mine.*
> *I choose you to watch, you to observe, you to control.*
> *You are mine, until I see another way.*
> *My power will take you, my power will take you*
> *until I am done.*
> *No rest, no sleep.*
> *Look deep, look deeper.*
> *All is lost.*

Becky handed the email to Olly, who had been trying to read it over her shoulder. 'So, that parchment, in Polish, says the Mirror now owns you?'

'Yes. I have tried to get a prayer and instruction from my rabbi. I have looked online to see if anyone has a record of that thing anywhere. There is nothing. If what that letter says is true, I have a mirror with something inside it. A mirror I cannot get rid of. A mirror that may be linked with occult practices and a mirror that no one can say where it came from, apart from hearsay.'

'And when you tried to dump it, it just came back?' Olly was looking at the ebony scrollwork and wooden roses on each corner.

'Yes.'

Both Becky and Olly were silent. Neither now doubted the integrity of this quiet man, sitting in his antique shop in York. Becky was feeling more anxious by the minute. There were no smells and the light remained bright in the interior of the shop. She knew she had to go and look closely at the mirror.

'May I?' she asked Max, as she stood up and turned her head towards it.

'For God's sake, be careful, Miss Moran,' said Max, taking off his spectacles.

'God, indeed,' thought Becky as she slowly approached the Mirror. The ebony wood was gleaming, the aged patina of the glass reflecting the interior of the shop. As she looked, she thought she saw something move across the surface. The movement was so small, a flicker, it could just have been a trick of the light. Becky stood in front of it, face on, seeing her own reflection stare back.

As she peered into the glass, a handprint formed on the bottom right-hand corner. It was forming from the inside and the glass itself seemed darker, more opaque. The heat of the print left a clear impression. As Becky stared at it, another started to form beside it, this time much smaller, and was then joined by its pair: clearly a child's prints. The image started to fog, as though a mist was swirling from deep within. Becky caught her breath. Her own reflection was now indistinct. Yet another handprint formed, this one much larger and obliterating the first three. Then another. The handprints proliferated from inside the surface of the glass at astonishing speed, making Becky take a step back. Now the interior surface of the mirror was covered with handprints, the earlier ones fading slightly only to be replaced quickly by fresh ones. Her face disappeared. Becky looked at the Mirror, hazy with imprints, darkening with a shadowy mist. Time seemed to have slowed down, like the frames of a film – of reality itself – winding down and out.

She watched as the handprints faded and the mist boiled, swirling towards the surface of the glass, emerging from somewhere deep inside and towards her. It reminded Becky of fog in the headlights of a car when all visibility is obscured, when slivers of light cut through the mist and make the refractions of the electric light dance.

She stared, almost mesmerised, and saw the ebony frame moving, the fretwork expanding, the ebony roses, once closed and exquisitely carved on each corner of the frame, flowering, opening, twisting. They looked obscene in their blackness – death flowers, grotesque, deriding the beauty of their origin, flowers crafted to sit on an ancient coffin and mock the dead.

The Mirror appeared to expand, growing to fill the blank wall. The glass was now black and bubbling with mist and dark shadows. All the handprints had disappeared. There was no sound. The mist swirled, and Becky squinted as she saw a shape forming. With no haste at all, the dark shadows seemed to settle into form behind the glass and, as if by some unseen command, the wooden roses, now overblown and pulsating, their blackness deep and ripe, bent on their stems towards the glass. They stretched inwards from their anchor points on the outer corners of the frame. Becky knew that to be touched by them would be poison; their putrid sap dripping acid and deadly ichor would eat away her flesh. In the second she took to register that thought, an image formed in the glass.

There was a face, not her face – please not – in the mirror. A face of soft folds of flesh, built from layers of mist. A face of ancient, knowing, corrupt, heinous flesh. A face that was once female but from which age had erased anything feminine. The mist formed sparse wisps of hair, long and curling away, formed out of black fog, moving like the body of a snake out of the mist-formed skull into thin tails of smoke. The sexless features formed a mouth, which was speaking, chanting soundlessly.

The face was moving closer and closer to the surface, angry yet triumphant, yearning, seeing Becky – seeing her – silently shouting its mantra, commanding, inviting, wanting just to reach the surface of the glass and reach through to take Becky by the hand and drag her, screaming, down, down, down to where they all were… Becky leant towards the mirror, her hand raised. The glass rippled as Becky's fingers hovered over the blackness.

CHAPTER SEVEN

Max started to move towards Becky, seeing Olly ahead of him almost leap towards her. He was younger and faster. Max shouted 'No!' as he saw the young woman's hand move towards the mirror's black surface. As if the scene was taking place in slow motion, he saw Olly glance for a split second at the mirror, at the same time embracing Becky Moran in a move which reminded Max of a rugby tackle. The younger man grabbed her outstretched arm, wrapped both his own arms around her and brought her to the floor.

Max Smythe dropped to his knees in sheer panic and relief. He looked up and caught a fleeting glimpse of the thing in the glass, the thing that was in his dreams every night. The eyes looked straight at him. Max looked away, his arm protecting his face. All three lay in a heap on the floor. The front door opened.

'I say, are you all right?' A North Yorkshire matron in tweed was in the doorway. 'I wanted to look at that boot scraper in the window. Do I need to call an ambulance?'

In the aftermath, no ambulance was sent for, but the matron did wonder whether there was some strange sex act going on in that antique shop in Swinegate. She had seen her chickens act very strangely around the cockerel in the hen house often enough. The older man got to his feet; it was a slow process, but he showed her the boot scraper, although she couldn't help looking over his shoulder at the young couple as they went to the back of the shop. The matron was curious to see what they were doing. It could have been an orgy she had just interrupted and, never mind it was lunchtime, these things happened.

Olly and Becky sat at the desk while Max saw to his customer. Becky was blinking, pale, and feeling confused.

'What do you mean, there were handprints and a face?' Olly asked. 'Are you all right, Becky? We just saw you staring at that mirror, then you were reaching out to it and when I called your name you didn't even respond.'

'How long was I there?' asked Becky.

'About half a minute,' said Olly. 'Max knew there was something wrong. He was desperate you didn't touch the mirror. You didn't, did you?'

Becky shook her head. She didn't tell Olly that the thing in the Mirror had seen her and had it reached her, touched her, she would have been dragged in. She knew that was so. She knew that whatever ability she now had made her susceptible to what was in there. Olly would probably have lost his temper, wouldn't have believed her anyway. She looked up at Max Smythe, who was clearly trying to get the woman out of the shop and see if Becky was all right and knew she couldn't help him. In fact, she had almost not been able to help herself.

'Thank you, Olly,' Becky said, composing herself. 'Can we get out of here? I need a drink and I want to get back to Cambridge.'

'Okay,' said Olly. 'Sure you're all right?' Becky nodded, looking away. As the matron left, Max came over to see Becky. Olly said she was fine and, yes, they would like to film the story of the Mirror. Max stared at Becky, nodding.

'What did you see?' he asked.

'Nothing,' lied Becky. 'I just had a moment.' She stood up and took Max's hand. 'Please don't worry about me, just look after yourself. Can you hide that thing? I don't think anyone will buy it and it's spooking you out. Wrap it up and hide it somewhere is my advice.'

'So, you did see something?' Max asked.

Becky shook her head. 'Take it down, Mr Smythe.'

Olly thanked him profusely for his time and said he would be back in touch when he had the filming schedule sorted. Max kept looking at Becky.

'You promised you would help me,' he said.

'I can't.' Becky looked away. She needed to leave.

As they left the shop, Max Smythe stood at the door and waved them off. He looked terrified.

The next day, Fabien reported his father missing. The police were puzzled as the doors to the shop were all locked from the inside and the new steel shutters had been lowered. They'd had to break in. The alarm had not been set and the shop was empty.

Fabien knew his father had been expected home at six. He also knew how meticulous his father was about the shop's security. Once the police had broken into the shop, Fabien saw there'd been a customer that afternoon who had bought an antique ring and left a deposit, all neatly documented in his father's hand in the sales ledger. The till receipt for the deposit was marked at 4.30 p.m. Fabien stood by the desk in the shop as the police searched it, feeling desperate; his eyes kept going back to the mirror on the wall by the door.

No one had seen Max Smythe again that afternoon.

The police launched an enquiry and Fabien and his mother were frantic. Rabbi Moyen came to the house, his face pale. Fabien asked him if his father had said anything to him about the mirror or his state of mind, but the rabbi had looked away and murmured, 'No, nothing. Fabien, come on now – you don't want your mother to think Max was in any way delusional, do you?' Fabien shook his head and accepted the rabbi's prayers.

Fabien took down the Mirror a week after his father had disappeared, sure – really sure – that this antique was connected in some way. As he wrapped it in a blanket to carry it down to the storage cellar, he noticed a man-sized handprint on the corner of the glass. It looked as though it were made from the inside. Fabien dropped the antique in the corner of the cellar and ran back upstairs as fast as he could.

Bert Brookings looked at the picture of Becky Moran in the Saturday edition of the *Daily Mail* and banged his fist down on her face. Bert was in his remote farmhouse on the edge of the Brecon Beacons. He was eating his wholemeal toast and organic honey and enjoying his green tea when that woman's face stared up at him from his morning newspaper. Bert had long thought of Becky Moran as some sort of spiritual nemesis: a pretender to his spiritual crown, a pretender with her own radio show, when he couldn't get so much as a split second on the media, not even on BBC local radio, never mind a place on a chat show sofa. Bert's indignation made his chest expand under his black towelling bathrobe, which was embroidered all the way down the back with a unicorn (naturally). Bert banged his fist again on the black and white image of the insipid redhead.

His Astral Enchantment fans would have been astonished at this fit of pique. Love was the answer, surely? Bert's followers were legion. Email subscribers and avid watchers of his YouTube channel, Astral Enchantment, the devoted arrived at his workshops (next one in Cleckheaton: 'Loving Yourself the Astral Way') clutching their money and their hopes of finding their Third Eye, of catching the Astral Express to self-love and understanding, and – this was the biggie – of being healed of their cancers, diabetes, multiple sclerosis, and arthritis, all of which Bert claimed he could cure by laying on his large, warm, heavily tattooed hands.

In America, Bert filled halls on the spiritual circuit, where he was a huge celebrity and coining it in. But in the UK, a more sceptical public did not yearn to catch the Astral Express quite so readily, and a vocal medical profession made it clear that ditching their drugs and radiotherapy to rely on fraudulent healing by a man called Bert with warm hands, was at best optimistic and at worst downright dangerous.

Bert had multiple testimonials online: 'Love cured me!', 'Harness the unicorn within!', 'You are loved!', all with images of Bert's imposing frame, muscles bulging under his short-sleeved Abercrombie & Fitch t-shirt, shaven head gleaming, bright blue eyes staring straight into the camera. He wore contacts to enhance the blue and he was aware that the stare had been likened to that of a psychopath eyeing his prey. He would welcome the viewer to Astral Enchantment, telling them that they were '*extraordinary*!' They were '*loved*!' They were going to have all their 'heart's *desires*!' (a slight wink there from Bert), and everything was just a subscription away. The video would then cut to testimonials by the converted, the healed, and the grateful. These were mainly Americans who wore Bert's signature t-shirt (which he sold at a huge profit to the adoring and were churned out in a sweatshop in Bangladesh), dark blue with his silver logo, a big A and E spelling out the words Astral Enchantment with a starburst and rays of light radiating out under the words. The rest of the testimonials he had written himself.

Bert was particularly proud of his video of a black woman with a five-year-old girl wriggling on her knee, telling the camera that Bert and Astral Enchantment had cured the child of a rare form of leukaemia and how the doctors somewhere in Alabama had no scientific explanation. It was one of Bert's top-rated online videos. The final frame showed Bert, eyes closed and with his hands on the little girl's head, proclaiming, 'By the Power of the Unicorn and Astral Enchantment, I have set you free!' The child in the film looked at him as if he were about to explode in a ray of astral starlight.

That final shot had required six takes, and the child had duly been presented with the puppy her momma and Bert had promised her.

Bert worked out. He was all muscle and steroids. Body art covered his arms, legs, chest, and back. He had just stopped short of having his skull inked. Naked, he could flex his powerful back and make the elaborate and highly stylised tattoo of the unicorn move as if galloping, and the horn flex. He pumped iron and he lifted weights and he shaved his head each morning, enjoying the buzz of the electric blades as they erased the balding hair pattern. He slipped in the blue contacts and tilted what he knew was a chiselled jaw. He told himself he could have been a quarterback in a top American football team with his build, although, in England, many might say he looked more like a bouncer down the Locarno on a Saturday night. All he needed was the black greatcoat and gloves.

Bert came from the backstreets of Cardiff. From a poor family, he had discovered that fists were a good way to get what he wanted. He was a bad lad, several brushes with the law soon labelling him a delinquent despite his intelligence. Rather than just being a bully, he could have been a darn good lawyer if he'd only realised that passing exams may have got him somewhere; or, if conventional religion had got hold of him, a great hellfire and damnation preacher in the southern states of America.

Instead, he got to share a room in a detention centre when he was sixteen with a con called Taff, who was on some new self-improvement course which involved looking at himself in their grimy mirror every morning and repeating mantras like, 'I am a wonderful person. People love me. I can achieve anything...' Naturally, Bert gave Taff a good thumping the first morning he watched him talk to himself in the mirror. But the seeds were sown for building a self-improvement empire. Astral

Enchantment came later after Bert overdid a bit of crystal meth on a Monday night down Tiger Bay. Bert never did illegal drugs again (steroids didn't count, even if the means of getting them might not quite have been legal), but his astral path was clear.

The rest, as they say, was history.

The healing power was harder to explain. Whilst Bert knew how to use his own backstory of bad-lad-turned-good to great effect in his ministry – *Astral Enchantment Saved Me!* – there was no doubt that when he laid his hands on the sick and the weak, something really happened. Bert felt the power flow out of his body and his clients also felt a great heat and some relief.

Of course, the sick beat a path to his door, desperate for anything to ease pain or fear, usually because whatever their doctors had prescribed was useless. Bert whipped them up with *The Power of the Unicorn!* and told them not just that he and the universal spirit loved them but that they loved themselves. By the time the large tattooed hands had touched the afflicted, they were quivering with anticipation and could feel a power course through their body, leaving the session in a daze of gratitude.

Many bought the expensive 'remote healing' sessions in which Bert picked a time and told his client to lie down in a darkened room. He would focus his Astral Enchantment on them, and they would feel the healing and *The Power of the Unicorn!* This would work anywhere in the world, he claimed. The truth was that Bert took the money and was more likely to be pressing weights in his home gym or be down the pub. Hardly anyone ever complained – and if they did, Bert would say with huge sorrow that the client clearly didn't believe enough. He never gave refunds, but reluctantly would offer another remote healing session at a slightly reduced rate (after all, 'You didn't believe enough but I still love you!').

Astral Enchantment was an investment every way you looked at it.

He registered the business in Panama, where fewer questions were asked, while living on a small farm on the borders of the National Park with a few chickens and a barn. This was the green space he had longed for as a child in Cardiff. The farmhouse wasn't particularly clean, but he had a small state-of-the-art studio for filming and his healing sessions took place in a room he hired in central London, not far from the British Museum. He had a professional gym at the farmhouse and ran his online empire from a tiny, very unprofessional office. Here he wrote his subscriber emails, badly spelled, the latest being headed '*HOW MUCH MOR CAN I LOVE YOU?*' Bert went on to speak of his eternal gratitude that his universal messages were being heard here on planet Earth, and did his readers know there were two-for-one offers on the workshops running up until Christmas? The email ended with the huge assurance that Bert '*loves you with evry atom of his being!*' just before a link to buy tickets for the Cleckheaton gig.

Most people assumed that Bert had a huge team working for him but in fact, he did it all himself. Being a peddler of unicorn healing was a lonely business and best kept private. Bert hated the fact that Becky Moran had all that support, especially from Hugh Jolly. He wanted to wipe both of them off the face of the Earth. And sitting in the cluttered kitchen of his farmhouse that Saturday morning, his mood was darkening further.

However, the long-term use of steroids had caused two unfortunate problems that Bert felt were hindering his rise to fame. Firstly, his penis was now very small, so he had taken to putting a sock down his trousers, two if he was working a festival. Also, the drugs had raised the timbre of Bert's voice, resulting in a sound that didn't match the body. Add to that a strong Welsh accent and Bert had to work quite hard to lower the lilting squeal for public consumption. It was not quite *Hi di Hi* but nowhere near Richard Burton. When he was angry – and that picture of Becky Moran in the *Daily Mail* was making him very, very angry – the voice came out high-pitched and feminine.

'Shit!' he squeaked. Then, with a nervous look around in case anyone had heard him sound like a castrato, he repeated, 'Shit,' much lower. He cleared his throat, flexed his muscle-bound arms, and began to rip up the newspaper, smiling grimly as he tore Becky Moran into shreds.

CHAPTER EIGHT

The following Friday, Becky Moran was in the Cube, getting ready for that evening's edition of *Medium Wave*. Iris, her mother, had called from Leeds to check the power wouldn't go off again tonight as she had some mushroom vol-au-vents in for her guests and had made a cheesecake. Becky was busy and wanted to get her mother off the phone.

'See you and Dad in Leeds next week. I'm up for some readings – and if not, I have your tickets for the Dominion Theatre a week next Sunday for the show. Is Dad going to come this time?'

Becky and her father had a strained relationship. He knew she was a fake – Becky wryly wondered what he would think now, after the events of the last seven days – and he despised her career, fame or not. He blamed Hugh Jolly for diverting his daughter from a proper job, especially as she had a Cambridge degree. He managed how he felt by not listening to her radio show and allowing Iris to revel in Becky's celebrity by default. In short, he was angry that his beautiful daughter was exploiting grief and play acting.

'Oh, he'll come. We've booked a hotel – never mind your Dad.' Iris was unconcerned. 'Shall I wear that powder-blue trouser suit I got in Debenhams? For the Dominion show?'

'Perfect, Mum. Bye now.'

Becky put her mobile phone down on the desk. The production office was busy this Friday afternoon, with rows of journalists on the phones, fixing up guests and typing notes. Olly was still refusing to discuss what had happened a week ago at the Cube when the lights went out. And Becky was refusing to discuss what she had seen in that antique mirror in York two days before.

She knew that Max Smythe had never left his shop that afternoon. She knew that had she just touched that mirror, it would have sucked her down, down, down with the others. Her stomach clenched in fear when she remembered that face, the old hag's face, chanting at her, wanting her. She had liked Max, but she knew he would never be found.

Becky felt a mix of fear and sadness when she thought about Max's disappearance. Becky's rational mind knew there had to be an explanation as to why that vibrant, kind man had vanished. A few days ago, before something unexplained had entered her life – changed it – when she touched the crystal of John Dee, Becky would have had several theories about a missing antique dealer in York, one who claimed he had a mirror that turned black and was capable of attaching itself to a human being. Now, in this world, which Becky felt was being glimpsed through an open door to the paranormal, her rationality was diminishing. Becky was looking at the production notes for tonight's guests. She was dressed in a fitted black dress, slightly off the shoulder, and her customary black Louboutins with the red soles. She looked down the running order: John X was back with his story of being a psychic spy for the CIA and his remote viewing of everything from Cold War targets to the Ark of the Covenant.

They had a man in – he was using the name Henry – who claimed to own the legendary Thirteenth Crystal Skull, and Olly said he was bringing his own security guard with him as the artefact was priceless and powerful. Henry claimed that dark forces were after the skull – hence the anonymity. I certainly hope not, thought Becky wryly. These skulls were usually very good fakes, but Henry claimed he had the most powerful one of all. Her notes told her that the skulls were often said to be hewn by an ancient Mesoamerican civilisation – or supposedly from Atlantis. The British Museum had their own, a prized exhibit. Henry said, predictably, that his was extraterrestrial, hidden by the Aztecs before the Spanish conquest. Its supernatural powers were unparalleled.

Olly had the plastic copy of the skull, which Henry had sent him, sitting on his desk. It was remarkably good – clear plastic and with full detail: hollowed-out eye sockets and teeth set in the jawline. What made this one interesting was the elongated cranium, so that it looked like an alien skull. Olly thought it added a touch of the macabre, a bit of *Hamlet* to the Divine Diva office. All week, Hugh had been rubbing the other-worldly plastic head as he walked past it. 'For luck,' Hugh had said, as his

Gucci shirt sleeve swept the gleaming cranium, Hugh's pale hand darting out to touch the shiny, creepily long dome.

'How do you know it's not cursed?' Sarah had asked. 'In my culture, a skull is voodoo.' Her eyebrows rose, and she stared at Hugh intently. Hugh's hand had shot away and he'd gone pale. Olly had just laughed.

Next on her list – and, at this, Becky shook her head in exasperation – was Bert Brookings, Unicorn Healer and all-around Welsh thug. She knew Olly was under editorial pressure to accommodate a big advertiser with an interview on her show, but she found Brookings's claims of healing offensive. Plus, he was semi-literate, and she had always sensed a violent nature emanating from him. That was going to be an interesting interview. He should have been in later in the month but the guest who had been scheduled for tonight – an American woman called Yolanda who'd written a book on sexually aggressive extraterrestrials allegedly abducting farmers in Idaho to perform unnatural acts on them and their dairy herds – had had to cancel. Her publisher had said it was a pure conspiracy that Yolanda's UK visa had been denied. Olly thought it may be more to do with her criminal record for running a hydroponic plant in Boise, Idaho, and selling cannabis to local high school students. So, Bert's interview had been brought forward. Olly had said he didn't even hesitate at the change of date.

I bet, thought Becky.

Becky turned back to her notes, prepared by Sarah, on the phone guests for tonight's readings. These normally gave Becky what she needed to amaze the 'caller' with her prowess as a medium. These clients were known as phone-outs at *Medium Wave*, but on air, it sounded as if they had called in. Well, they had originally, but Sarah researched their background for Becky before they were called back some weeks later and the medium's reading sounded as fresh and spontaneous as was possible.

Tonight, there was Mary from Dagenham, whose brother had committed suicide in May. Sarah had full notes on where and how, gleaned from the local papers. Mary wanted to know why. The other caller would be Stephen. He was something in the City and wanted to connect with his best friend who'd gone missing in Borneo on a hiking trip a year ago and hadn't been seen since.

Sarah knew that Stephen was bonking the presumed widow and had been, even before said best friend took his rucksack and hiking boots on a very long walk into the jungle. Guilt drove Stephen. Plus, he wanted to marry this woman who had no idea if her husband was dead or alive. Becky knew she wouldn't need Sarah's notes now, anyway. She just knew the spirits would be there.

Sarah was treating Becky as if light shone from every orifice, a creature to be revered in her psychic glory. She had brought Becky a picture of herself and her dead twin, taken when they were five. Becky recognised the brother instantly, as he had appeared next to Sarah at the meeting in Cambridge that Monday. Sarah had cried a bit more, hugged and thanked Becky again. The waves of mothballs coming off her clothes were as overpowering as ever. Today, Sarah was wearing a pink batwing jumper and red leggings. They were both from Oxfam. The yellow boots were from a car boot sale in Hackney.

Hugh Jolly was due at the Cube in a couple of hours. Olly had called him and explained what had happened in York. Hugh had gone very quiet. He had not sounded pleased when Olly said the family wouldn't give permission to film the Mirror as they were distraught that Max was missing. His son, Fabien, had called Olly to ask what had happened on Wednesday afternoon, the day Max disappeared. Olly said nothing had happened; he certainly wasn't going to describe Becky Moran standing transfixed in front of the glass. He just told Fabien that Max had seemed upset about the antique from Poland and that he hoped he would be found soon. Fabien had thanked him and said he appreciated his concern. Olly wished the family the best of luck and said Fabien should call him with any news.

Olly didn't think he would hear from that family ever again.

Becky had changed her mind and stayed in London when she and Olly got back to King's Cross from York. She couldn't face going back to the mews house in Cambridge just yet. She had checked into a small boutique hotel in Covent Garden, modern, well lit, and comforting; it was her hotel of choice when in the capital. The last two nights, Becky had slept undisturbed, bathed in white light in her dreams. She knew her life had changed. She felt like a newborn. She continued to see spirits everywhere: the girl on Reception at the hotel had her mother standing behind her, smiling with pride. The spirit had smiled at Becky and put her hand (though not quite there) on her daughter's shoulder as if to protect her. Becky had decided to test her new theory with a complete stranger.

'You know I'm a medium?' she'd said to the young woman, who was taking her credit card details. 'Yes, Miss Moran, I always listen to your radio show.' She smiled across the desk.

'Your mother has passed, hasn't she?' asked Becky. The receptionist looked startled and then sad.

'Yes, ten years ago, when I was twelve.' Becky looked at the spirit, who told her that her girl was an amazing daughter and that she was with her all the time. 'Tell her I love her,' said the spirit, 'please tell her how much.' Becky did so and described the blue dress the spirit was wearing, and then asked the young woman to show her the locket she wore every day. The receptionist lifted the chain from around her neck, hidden by her blouse, in astonishment.

'That has a lock of your mum's hair inside,' Becky told her. 'Your mum says you have worn it since the day she died. Is that true?' The woman nodded slowly.

'How could you know that?' she asked. Becky smiled, her grey eyes soft and gentle.

'Your mum just told me. She misses you very much, but you just need to know she is with you now and always.'

Becky now knew she could connect with the spirits she could see. By acknowledging they were there – well, ethereal, not quite there, but ready to come forward – she could hear them and see them. Becky had already learned that by putting up a mental barrier she could control that connection. That was a relief, because the world would be crowded and unpredictable otherwise.

What Becky was frightened of, though, were not the benign entities she could tune in to. It was the dark ones. That door to another dimension and what may lie there. What was in that darkness and what did it want with her?

Sarah was mesmerised by the polka dots on Aiden O'Conner's bow tie. Aiden O'Conner was the boss at The Voice of Britain. His stomach was prodigious. Some very young, very unwise trainee journalist had once set a stopwatch on it. The stomach entered a room precisely half a second before the rest of him. With shirt buttons straining, the belly would lead the way. Known to wobble with indignation and bounce on the rare occasions that Aiden laughed, the belly even dominated when he wore a dinner jacket; it gave the impression it was an alien entity, about to burst through the black cloth before destroying anything it saw in a bath of acid.

Today, the bow tie was decorated with red polka dots. Aiden hand tied it, though getting near to the full-length mirror was hampered by the belly barrier. Aiden wore a bow tie every day. It was well known that he considered it to be his style icon, his mark of eccentricity: preppy, distinctive, authoritative. He had one in every colour. He favoured the red, probably because he thought it lifted the sallowness of the dark rings under his eyes and took attention away from his double chin. Sarah could tell he thought the look was jaunty, though she thought he had the look of a demonic clown about to devour small children during a matinee under the Big Top.

Sarah was on her way to the Green Room to check that the hospitality was sorted for the guests this evening, and then she would be meeting Becky to run through their notes for the show tonight. O'Conner was on the prowl. Sarah suspected it was Becky he may like to devour and knew she should try and deflect Aiden from his search. He had thumped his way down the corridor at the Cube, the dense mass of stomach barring Sarah's way. But, unlike many at the radio station, Sarah wasn't intimidated by the Irishman. She worked for Hugh and Becky, not O'Conner directly, and had known enough bully bosses in her time. Sarah met his gaze, peered at the polka dots, squinted, and then looked back at Aiden's face.

'What?' she asked.

'Where is she?' demanded Aiden.

'Which "she" are you referring to?'

'Becky, unless you have Mother Teresa hidden in there.' He jerked his head towards the Green Room.

'Oh, were you looking for Mother Teresa? She died the same week as Princess Di, 1997 I believe, and she isn't in there either. I don't know where Becky Moran is, Aiden. I am not the psychic, and nor do I have her electronically tagged. When I see her, I shall tell her you were looking for her. Anything else?'

Aiden's eyes narrowed. Most staff at The Voice of Britain would have been clutching rosary beads and kissing their bottoms goodbye at this point, had they had the courage to give as much back to the boss. Sarah wasn't kissing anything. She held her gaze, whilst also managing to show some disdain for the polka dots. O'Conner nodded curtly, turned, and walked away. Sarah mouthed an expletive at his broad, departing back. And then, just for good measure, she mouthed another.

Becky was looking at the large crystal skull with the elongated cranium, which was placed on a black velvet bag on the felt-covered table in her studio. The *On Air* light was on, and *Medium Wave* had been broadcasting for ten minutes.

Nick was back, driving the control desk in Ops, and Olly was producing the show through the glass. Hugh was standing behind Olly. He looked sober. He had arrived at the Cube at six o'clock and escorted Becky to a coffee shop in Covent Garden. He wanted assurances that she had not gone stark staring mad. Becky reassured him, explaining that, yes, she could see spirits as clearly as she had seen his father last week. She passed over the details of what had happened in York, not quite meeting Hugh's eyes, and nor did she describe in detail what had happened in Cambridge at the mews house the previous Saturday night. Hugh said ticket sales for the Sunday show at the Dominion were good and their online hits had rocketed since that piece in the *Daily Mail*. Subscriptions to her online blogs were also up and they had a new Internet advertiser. There was a lot at stake for them both.

'Are we okay?' asked Hugh.

'Absolutely,' answered Becky, with a conviction she did not feel.

She had walked into the studio half an hour before her show started at eight this Friday night. Becky had a flashback to the events of a week ago when the lights went out, but now everything was as it should be. This studio was a place Becky loved. The microphone was waiting, not a coiled-up snake waiting to strike, and the computer screen was glowing softly, waiting for her to log on. A glass of water with ice had been placed on the table for her by Sarah. There was order here. Nothing to be scared of at all. Becky looked at the glass wall of the Cube that overlooked Covent Garden. It was dark by now and the glow of the street lights and restaurants across the road was as comforting as usual.

Becky, wearing headphones so she could hear herself and Olly if he spoke to her, was looking at the crystal skull as Henry talked about extraterrestrials. The security guard stood silently beside Henry. Hugh had seen them both in the Green Room before *Medium Wave* went on air and told Olly the minder was 'built like a brick shithouse, with arms like tree trunks'. The brick shithouse now standing at Henry's side was alert and poised to brain any would-be robber who may run into the radio studio and try to steal the skull. It weighed so much that any thief would have to be fitter than a shot putter even to lift it.

The skull was magnificent. Made from smooth, flawless, transparent quartz crystal, it looked like a block of ice formed from the purest mineral water. The bones and mandibles were beautifully etched. The eye sockets were deep-set and oval, larger than one would imagine in a normal skull. The cheekbones were sharp and elongated. Light glittered over the quartz surface, creating shadows of its own, deep in the solid recesses of the clear mass. The *On Air* light cast a crimson glow where it touched the dome, and it was that extended, smooth cranium that made this skull so striking. Not too much of a stretch to imagine an alien, a so-called Grey, inhabiting a skeleton such as this, with an exoskeleton of strange, mud-coloured elastic skin and flat, black eyes. You could imagine this entity hovering in a flying saucer somewhere near Roswell or abducting bewildered Texans and sending them back to Earth with futuristic chips embedded in their red necks.

Olly noted that Twitter was trending @MediumWave #crystalskull. The pictures he had posted of the skull were being shared everywhere on social media. He grinned. The advertisers would love that.

Henry, the owner of this strange artefact, looked like a Geography teacher in a third-rate free school somewhere in the Midlands. He had a sheen of perspiration on his face, a straggly beard, thick spectacles, and an even thicker Brummie accent. He sniffed frequently. Hugh suspected the overuse of white powder. He knew a cokehead when he saw one. Henry's suit was Armani, however, and the shoes were handmade by Church. Becky also noticed the Patek Philippe watch and wondered where the money came from. Listening to the story of the skull, she also wondered whether this man's imagination wasn't so far off the scale that he may need sectioning.

'It's embedded,' Henry told her. 'The power of the Thirteenth Skull. It is tens of thousands of years old and not created by any human hand, but by the crystallised consciousness of advanced beings, aliens who came to Earth and left this,' his hand touched the skull, 'as their legacy. It's proof that we are all made by an extraterrestrial civilisation.'

'Not made by a creator, then?' asked Becky. 'Or are we not a result of Darwinian evolution? Is it your belief that whatever made this skull is responsible for the evolution of the human species?'

Henry's eyes lit up. 'Yes, yes! This is their calling card, their legacy, their transmitter to the Mother Ship.'

'But Henry,' Becky's voice was soft and deceptively sweet as she spoke into the microphone, 'you have no proof, have you? Most crystal skulls were created by hand in the late nineteenth century and when they're examined under an electron microscope some of them clearly show marks from an electric diamond rotary saw. And Mesoamerican myths don't refer to any crystal skulls. Even the one in the British Museum is acknowledged as modern antique, a fake. There are many of them. These skulls are fascinating – they are pretty, definitely intriguing, even works of art. But not much else.'

Henry visibly bristled. 'This skull is a computer. It can record energy and vibrations and it transmits human history back to the aliens who created it. They have shown me where they came from and chosen me to take their message to mankind. They have made me their Earth-bound messenger and endowed me with material wealth.'

Henry was sounding rather petulant at being questioned about the glittering skull. A few onlookers were standing outside, peering at the glass wall of the Cube and clearly intrigued by the large crystal object, gruesome though anatomically correct apart from that dome, sitting in front of Becky Moran.

'When the time is right, they will come back and claim it!'

'Where did you get it from, Henry? And when will the time be right?'

Henry looked shifty, shuffled a bit in his seat and sniffed again.

'It came to me, is all I can say. This is one of the thirteen. It is the largest and the most powerful. And when all thirteen skulls are reunited, then the aliens will return. I am appealing to those who have the other twelve skulls. They know who they are.' Henry rubbed his nose, as if it were itching, just on the septum. 'I appeal for them to come forward, so we can create the New World Order! The combined power of the skulls will project back into the cosmos. This is our destiny, mine and for all mankind!'

Henry's face was slick with sweat now. The security guard never moved a muscle. Olly and Hugh were watching Becky and the skull from the Ops room. Hugh was shaking his head, looking at Henry.

'That's a nutter in there,' he said to Olly. Olly smiled, looking at the bank of lights from callers flashing up on his console. The listeners were loving this.

'So... let me be clear,' said Becky. 'You won't tell me where this artefact came from or how you come to own it. You have not shown me any evidence of its provenance. I have only your word that this skull is not a fake, and I only have your word that it's some sort of alien transmitter in the shape of a skull. I need a bit more than that, Henry.'

'This skull has psychic powers and anyone who says they have extrasensory perception just has to touch it. You can feel the power.'

Becky, who wasn't sensing anything from the skull but was sensing a great deal about Henry, paused for effect, and then asked, 'May I touch it?'

Sarah, listening upstairs in the Green Room, caught her breath. She wondered what would happen when Becky touched that alleged powerhouse of psychic energy. She was slightly distracted by the large hand of John X, which flexed in anticipation as he helped himself to another sugar doughnut. Sarah glanced at Bert Brookings, perched at the edge of the sofa, with his clothes stretched over his muscles like a caged gorilla in fancy dress. He was eating a custard cream and looked as if he was about to dunk it in his coffee. He seemed full of nervous energy and steroids, pumped up because, Sarah assumed, he was actually in the Cube. Sarah turned back to the speaker to listen to what Becky would say next. She jumped when Bert's deep Welsh voice cut across the programme feed.

'Have you felt the Power of the Unicorn?' he asked her. She turned towards him, annoyed that he was interrupting her enjoyment of the show. Sarah loathed Brookings as much as Becky did.

'Where have you parked it?' she asked. 'Tottenham Court Road?'

Bert muttered an insult under his breath and Sarah turned her attention back to the speaker.

'I invite you,' said Henry, 'to feel the force of the crystal skull.' He waved his hand, rubbed his nose again, and sniffed. He sat back in his seat and smiled slyly at Becky over his thick spectacles, leaning back from his microphone.

Becky Moran reached out her hand towards the skull.

CHAPTER NINE

Becky's hand hovered over the crystal skull, not quite touching it. She looked at Henry.

'More in a moment. Don't forget to follow the show on Twitter @MediumWave. But first, these messages,' said Becky, speaking into her microphone. Olly nodded to hit the commercial break. The *On Air* light switched off. Becky slipped off her headphones, knowing her microphone was mute and that the only people who could hear her were those in the studio with her right now.

'Henry – I know that's not your real name – I am going to touch this skull. But first, you need to know that I am aware of who you really are. You are a drug dealer from Solihull. A successful one, judging by your clothes, and I suspect that the minder,' Becky nodded at the brick shithouse, 'usually acts as your bodyguard. But I can also see a spirit behind you, a young man who overdosed on some crap you sold him last week. He died horribly. He says you cut the heroin with plaster. And what's more, some Columbian is after you for missed payment on a consignment you took possession of last week. Personally, I don't care, but I am warning you that when that red light goes back on I shall be quite honest that this thing,' Becky waved at the skull and then pointed at Henry, 'and you are fakes. I know you want fame and people to believe you have a supernatural artefact of power. Time to start praying that the aliens are listening.'

Henry's jaw dropped open as Becky put her headphones back on. Olly buzzed 'Five seconds' in her ear.

'This is *Medium Wave* on The Voice of Britain,' said Becky. 'Tonight, a crystal skull that is claimed to have been hewn by aliens and, what's more, a claim that the extraterrestrials who made the skull actually created the human race. Henry – not his real name – is here. He owns this skull. He tells me it has extraordinary power and anyone with a gift like mine will feel it instantly. So, I am about to touch the artefact and see if it has any power.'

Becky paused.

Her hand slowly touched the skull. Nothing, not even a vibration.

'It feels cold and smooth,' said Becky. 'However, I sense no power, alien or otherwise. Henry, in my psychic opinion this skull is nothing more than a huge chunk of quartz. I suggest you take it, enjoy it, and, if what you say is true, I sincerely hope one day you can prove it. Thanks for being a guest on *Medium Wave* tonight.'

Olly hit a promo for The Voice of Britain Breakfast Show. The red light went out. Henry stood up, gesturing to his minder to put the skull back in its box, as Olly came through to escort him out. Henry was furious.

'You will regret this,' he hissed at Becky.

'As will you, when the Columbians find you,' replied Becky. Olly looked puzzled.

'Mary, the caller, is on next,' he said to Becky as Henry and the brick shithouse carried their alien skull through the door.

Aiden O'Conner wanted to meet John X. He had instructed Sarah to bring him to his executive suite after his appearance on *Medium Wave*, something Sarah found interesting, not least because O'Conner would not normally be in the Cube at this time on a Friday night. Maybe he was after twiddling his bow tie at Becky. Sarah rolled her eyes when the request came through to bring John X upstairs, because that involved escorting the American so-called psychic spy to the top floor while she was supposed to be doing her job as a runner for the radio show. She was also under the strictest instructions from Hugh to keep Bert Brookings as far away from Aiden as possible.

'Tip that Welsh idiot in the Thames, if you have to,' was the actual order. So now Sarah had to ensure that John X didn't tell Brookings, while they were both in the Green Room waiting to go on air, that Aiden was even in the building, never mind that only one of them had been summoned to a chinwag with a bow tie.

Maybe, if I put a broom up my backside, I can sweep the floor as well, thought Sarah, as she brought John X in the lift to the ground floor to be interviewed by Becky.

John X was morbidly obese. His underarms were ringed with sweat stains. His face, flaccid and layered with fat, still looked remarkably young but his breathing was laboured, and his colouring was high. Sarah thought he was not too far from a major cardiac arrest. In his early seventies, his sandy hair was sparse, and he was quietly spoken, polite – he called her 'ma'am' – and he had pale blue eyes which, frankly, looked haunted.

Aiden was intrigued by John X's story. Whilst he didn't believe a word of that supernatural mumbo jumbo that *Medium Wave* spouted on his radio station on a Friday night, the claims John X made about working for what, in the end, became known as the Stargate Project, did interest O'Conner. The Stargate Project had had several previous names since it was formed back in the 1970s, all its incarnations run by the CIA and the American military, paid for by both of them and the American Senate for twenty-five years. Although officially denied to this day, the project was born out of Cold War paranoia and a belief that the Russians had an army of psychics using their powers on the West. Well, on American military installations to be precise.

The story was that, in retaliation, American scientists had gathered a small group of military recruits with supposed psychic abilities, who were trained, monitored, and used in a top-secret unit conducting so-called paranormal experiments. Aiden didn't know if they moved magnets around, made bells ring, he guessed flash cards held up by a researcher, or were telepathic. He was aware many were what were known as 'remote viewers', able to sense unknown information about locations or events. By focusing on given coordinates, the viewer could sit in a room, hundreds, if not thousands, of miles away and 'see' that location. They often drew or described what they saw, and some were remarkably accurate. John X, who'd eventually had a complete breakdown, which he chronicled in his book, also claimed that he and others could remotely view events through space and time and that he'd witnessed key events in history, including the explosion on board Pan Am 103, the airline that exploded over Lockerbie in 1988.

O'Conner had covered a few covert CIA operations when he'd been a correspondent in Washington. He wanted some confirmation from John X that the Yanks had indeed used psychic spies to get one up on the rest of the world. Aiden waited, fingering his bow tie and listening to the mellifluous voice of Becky Moran on *Medium Wave*. O'Conner was smiling.

Becky talked over the jingle for the news at nine. After the last pip, the red light went off, giving her a five-minute rest as the newsreader read the bulletin before she began to broadcast the final hour of her show. Olly had been busy producing; the reaction to the show had been good tonight. Olly had taken dozens of calls about the crystal skull, mainly from people who wanted to know where they could see it, and from one man who said the aliens who created it were hovering over Lake Windermere right now. Olly thanked him for his call, shaking his head at the proliferation of wackjobs.

Hugh had met Bert Brookings in the Green Room before *Medium Wave* went on air. Brookings was wearing a tight black t-shirt and jeans, with two socks down his trousers for maximum effect. Normally, Hugh would have flirted with a well-built younger man, but he despised this pumped-up, uneducated peddler of Astral Enchantment. Brookings had shaken his hand with a vice-like grip and told Hugh straight out that he should hire him to present *Medium Wave* and let him communicate unicorn magic to the nation. Hugh had adopted his best Cambridge-acquired drawl and said in a cool voice that he already had a presenter for *Medium Wave*, but Bert should feel free to send in a showreel, so Hugh could consider his ability alongside everyone else who wanted to be a radio presenter. For good measure, Hugh asked him to be sure to include a unicorn, if he could find one able to speak.

Brookings's eyes had narrowed. He must have known when a posh gay bloke was taking the piss. He must also have known that Hugh and Becky were tighter than Morecambe and Wise.

Brookings told Hugh that Aiden O'Conner was interested in talking to him.

'Do make sure you compliment his bow tie,' was Hugh's sardonic reply. He knew Becky would be taking that lying unicorn and shoving it somewhere the hooves could dangle freely from inside Brookings's anatomy. He left the mouldy one to entertain tonight's guests. Sarah was banging coffee cups resentfully in a corner, muttering something about why Brookings was even on *Medium Wave*.

Becky sipped her iced water as the news was being read from a different studio in the Cube. She was feeling relaxed, connected to her new-found gift, and enjoying tonight's show, though she frowned at the thought of Bert Brookings, on in about half an hour. She stood up as John X was escorted into the studio by Olly.

'Hello,' said Becky and extended her hand. As his pudgy hand touched hers, Becky felt a jolt. She looked at John X, whose pale blue eyes had widened at the contact.

'You have it, you really have it,' John X said quietly as he withdrew the hand and nodded at Becky. 'Don't let the CIA get hold of you, Ms Moran,' he drawled in his west coast American accent, as he sat down with a microphone in front of him. 'You would be like a gold mine to them.'

Becky felt an enormous power emanating from John X. There was no sense of darkness, no fear, just a connection to this large, elderly American with such a remarkable story. She saw no spirits around him, but she could see an aura of whiteness surrounding him, a glow. That and a sense of sadness, a weariness, almost as if he were burned out with an energy that had allegedly taken him on some sort of psychic rollercoaster. Becky wondered if that soft, luminous aura wasn't a way of keeping spirits at bay, a sort of protective mantle. She made a mental note to visualise this if she ever needed it. Becky felt an empathy with this man; he too occupied a world that, in part, was revealed in a different dimension, and for a second Becky felt some comfort. Perhaps she wasn't totally alone in this supernatural wonderland. Plus, John X had survived. In those dark moments during the last week, Becky had considered quite seriously that she may not. John X was giving her hope.

'Ten seconds,' Olly buzzed in her ear. John X was looking intently at Becky.

'Welcome, you're listening to *Medium Wave* on The Voice of Britain.' Becky picked up after the opening jingle to her show, headphones on, speaking into her microphone. 'Coming up, a man who says the power of the unicorn can heal you. We're talking astral enchantment with Bert Brookings. But first, a man who claims he was a psychic spy for the American military and worked for the CIA, using his power to search for Russian military secrets during the Cold War. However, in his book *Remote Viewing through Space and Time*, John X says he can travel anywhere in history. And he claims he has seen the Ark of the Covenant. Welcome…'

'Thank you for having me on your show, ma'am,' said John X.

'If what you claim is true, why are you so sure the CIA won't want to stop you talking about what was, and still is, regarded as top secret? Denied at every level. After all, if you and others were in a unit of crack psychic spies, I have to assume that you are sworn to silence?'

John X smiled. 'The fact that the Stargate Project existed is a matter of record, approved and funded by the American government. I wrote my story because I believe that what we did – where we went, what we were asked to do, and the devastating effect our training and missions had on my health and that of my fellow psychic spies – that story needed telling. But I don't think the CIA is overly concerned. They just deny it all, say I'm mentally ill. And after all, Becky, you and I both know that while other dimensions exist… well, actually proving that? Very difficult. After all, it's a matter of belief. Your listeners believe you, don't they?'

'Yes,' replied Becky. 'But I can only tell them what spirits tell me. That is proof enough for many. How am I supposed to believe you can travel through space and time, even witness history, as you claim? Could it be that we find the idea of what you claim to be so… so magical, so out there… that we just gawp in wonder? Then you can blame a lack of any evidence on a conspiracy theory. You see my dilemma, don't you?'

Becky saw the phone lines were all busy, the switchboard lines flashing.

'Think of it this way,' replied John X, not in the least defensive. 'If you ask a Christian, a Jew, a Muslim to prove their God exists, could they? Those of faith talk about the power of prayer, they read their Bibles, their Torah, their Koran, and they tell their stories and try and live by the precepts of their faith. They will tell you their God is the true God. But can they show you their deity? Can they give you an address where they live? Can they take you to their front door and introduce you? No. But, for tens of millions, their faith is as real to them as you are. I can only tell you what I have seen, what I can do, and you will then decide if what I believe is real.' John X leaned forward towards Becky. 'Some of us have a gift. It is what we choose to do with it that matters. I choose to share my stories. And I've paid a price for my journey.'

Becky looked at John X with some sympathy. 'You had a complete mental breakdown, didn't you? Are you well now?'

John X looked away and Becky had to gesture to him to get him to turn back to the microphone. 'I was very ill, mentally ill, for a long time. I wrote my book as therapy. Yes, Ms Moran, I am recovered. Don't let my illness allow anyone to doubt me or what I have seen. Anyone can learn to be a remote viewer. Just put those words in a computer search engine. You can go on courses here in Britain, read the online chatter about how to "see" in a psychic sense.

'The Stargate Project was officially closed in 1995. But it is still run in America by two private companies, rather than being openly funded by the government. Be absolutely clear, it is still happening, and it is part of modern warfare. I was a psychic warrior.'

In Leeds, Iris was serving cheesecake and coffee while her guests raised their eyebrows at what John X was saying. 'Do you think he's a bit touched?' Iris asked her friend as she handed over the fresh cream. 'That man with the skull was very strange, but this one may need to go and see his doctor again. Poor thing. I'd never heard of this remote viewing. Is it like looking at a house for sale on the Internet? Coffee, everyone?'

Iris wished that Peter, Becky's dad, was here to enjoy the radio show. He had gone out at about seven to his book club. He just didn't understand what his daughter was up to and he clearly loathed Iris's friends, hanging on every word, gathered around the digital radio and cluttering up the kitchen every Friday night. He would go and sit in Roundhay Park in the rain if it meant getting out of the house if there were no book club to save him. As it was, he'd had a copy of *War and Peace* under his arm. Iris called after him to stay and listen for once in his sorry life. 'Save me some cheesecake,' he'd answered, closing the front door behind him.

Becky went to commercial break and the *On Air* light went out.

'Becky, you need to be very careful. Your gift is strong. It's not just the CIA who may want it. Are you battling something dark?' Becky nodded quietly. She trusted him. 'Fight it, Ms Moran. God, who or whatever that is, God help you.'

Becky felt that flash of fear. 'I don't know how.'

'Nor do I.' John X shook his head. He looked very sad. 'Nor do I.'

Olly buzzed 'Thirty seconds' and said it was sounding great. He gave her a four-minute warning of the phone reading coming next, with the man in search of his best friend lost in Borneo. Then Brookings. Becky looked through the glass at Olly and nodded. Hugh gave her the thumbs up and then made a rather rude, pumping gesture from the wrist in reference to Bert.

The *On Air* light went back on. Becky welcomed the audience back to *Medium Wave*, told them she would shortly be talking to Steve from London, searching for his missing friend in Borneo, and reminded the audience of the phone number to the studio if they wanted to call for an on-air reading. She continued her conversation with John X, who was now looking tired. When she asked about seeing the Ark of the Covenant, he began to drift, mumbling about mountains and hidden chambers, vague about the geographic location. Becky could see his narrative was faltering and Olly buzzed her to wind it up.

As another commercial break played out, Becky held out her hand to say goodbye to John X. His blue eyes were dull as he took her hand, though the aura was still strong around him. 'My medication makes me tired,' he explained. 'But you do need to be very careful, Ms Moran. Something happened here, didn't it, in this studio?' Becky nodded. 'I can feel something. Whatever it is, Becky, it is coming for you.'

Before she could ask what he meant, Olly came in to take John X out of the studio. John X stared back at Becky, the pale blue eyes sad as Olly led him out of the door, where Sarah was waiting to whisk him up to third floor Heaven to meet the God of the Cube in a bow tie, Aiden O'Conner.

Becky took a moment to look out of the window of the Cube; a small crowd of teenagers were smiling and waving at her from outside. She smiled back. That all felt very normal. Then she remembered that Brookings was on his way down from the Green Room, she remembered the fact she had just touched a lump of quartz in the shape of an alien skull, and she remembered she had just met a man who said he could travel through space and time and was a psychic warrior. Not to mention she now saw dead people everywhere and the psychic warrior had just warned her the dark was out to get her.

Normal suddenly felt a very long way away.

She looked down at the notes for Brookings. At the top of the pile of paper was a copy of Bert's latest email missive to the devoted, his final push for the healing event in Cleckheaton over the weekend.

Sadly, the header was *'DEEEP IN MY ARSENL OF UNICORN WEPONRY!'* Up in the production office earlier, Hugh had picked up the notes and howled with laughter.

'How deeep in the arse can you go!' he'd said in a very bad Welsh accent. He then read out some of the rest of it, camping up the Welshness and the terrible syntax. '*Super awesome!* We are going to be *full on*, boyos, so buckle up the seatbelts in overdrive and put your helmets on. The *Unicorn energy* will be pumping out of our space and it's going to be *radio rental!*' At that, Hugh guffawed some more. 'I'm *buzzing already!*' All of them had laughed. 'Is he for real?' Hugh had asked, handing the notes to Becky.

'His money is,' said Olly. 'That's why he's on. It will be the last time.'

Bert Brookings walked through the doors of Becky's studio and looked his nemesis straight in the eye. He had adjusted the two socks to enhance what the steroids had stolen and the muscles on his bare arms were thick ropes, rippling beneath the inked flesh. He had been practising keeping his voice low while rehearsing his Unicorn mantra and was clutching his notes, handwritten with diagrams, which looked like the work of a four-year-old. He had thought through every question Moran could possibly ask him and would use his notes to make sure he didn't miss a trick.

Becky stood up as he walked in. Her grey eyes were not warm, but she smiled in welcome. The news headlines were being read at nine thirty. Becky knew she had an interesting ten or so minutes coming up with Brookings. She took in the pumped-up frame and tight t-shirt and avoided staring at the impossibly bulging groin area.

'Hiya,' said Bert, gripping her hand so hard it hurt the bones.

Becky could recognise someone with special needs instantly. She had spent a couple of years with a high-functioning adult autistic. The Cambridge professor she had lived with as an undergraduate had been academically brilliant, handling his autism well. However, Becky knew from his behaviour that there was a fine line between facing the challenges of autism and being a complete git. Brookings was more git than muscle. He emanated a controlled violence, he was defensive and, she also knew from her research, he was delusional.

The Cambridge graduate with psychic ability from Leeds faced the uneducated bad boy from the back streets of Cardiff. It was as if battle lines were being drawn. Becky looked at the *On Air* light as it flicked on. Then she saw what was standing behind Brookings.

It took all her strength and professionalism not to stand up and run away, out of the studio and into the streets of Covent Garden.

CHAPTER TEN

Nick, the technician, saw Becky almost rise from her seat, still wearing her headphones. He remembered that she'd made a similar movement last Friday, just before the lights went out. He saw the console in front of him flicker and for a split second thought he was having a moment of déjà vu. Then everything settled back to normal. A power surge he thought, and went back to adjusting the levels and checking that his commercials were in order for the next ad break. Hugh and Olly watched Becky face off Brookings.

'She had better give him a hard time,' said Hugh. Olly just wanted a good, sparky interview. The wackjob devoted followers of the Unicorn would be tuned in everywhere, including the USA, where Brookings was often hailed as some kind of divine healing superstar. Ratings would be great tonight. He checked Twitter where @MediumWave #Unicorn was trending massively, but he stopped short of posting a cartoon unicorn on social media. There were limits. He settled for a picture of Bert, straining in an Astral Engagement t-shirt, lit from above and flexing his biceps.

Becky was staring at a space just behind Brookings. She knew the red light was on and she had to start the interview, but she was tense. Would the darkness return? She was waiting for that foul smell to fill the air. Brookings had no idea what Becky was looking at. He turned around. Nothing. He looked back at Becky, frowning quizzically, his bald head gleaming under the *On Air* light.

Becky could see a small, dark shape, the head bowed, behind Brookings. The mass appeared bent forward from the waist. The area where the face should have been was covered by the dark swathe of a cowl. It was perfectly still. Unlike the entities Becky had been seeing, or sensing for a week now, this one appeared as a solid mass. There was nothing fey or transparent here. Nothing benign either. The darkness of the shape seemed to absorb all the light around it, giving Becky the visual impression that the mass was like an ink stain on blotting paper, deep and permanent, throwing everything around it into sharp relief. Becky knew that the very space it occupied was a vacuum. As Brookings turned to look at the space Becky was staring at, the entity turned in perfect synchronicity, as if it were a black shadow, bound and stitched by invisible threads, muscle to muscle, skin cell to skin cell, joined to the human host. A black, carbonised attachment to Brookings, turning as he turned, not straightening or moving in any other way. The dark mass – beyond Becky's comprehension – existed in its conjoined dimension. Silent, absorbing all available light.

Olly clicked in her ear. She swallowed.

'Our last guest this evening is the internationally renowned healer and creator of astral enchantment. His "power of the unicorn" message has tens of thousands of followers both here in Europe and in North America.' Becky read the script Olly had written, fighting off the fear she felt from seeing the black shape and trying to sound sincere. 'Welcome, Bert Brookings, to *Medium Wave*.'

'It's about time I was here,' Bert said in his strong Welsh accent, sounding belligerent. Becky could sense the man in front of her expected her to be more welcoming, to make him feel comfortable, as was her role and his right from his interviewer during her live programme. She could see Bert's aggression; he looked as if he were up for a fight. Her usual control in her studio was being eroded – not by the pugnacious Welshman, but by what she could see attached to him. Becky was terrified.

'The Power of the Unicorn to the world!' Bert raised his arm and punched the air, completely unaware that the black shape behind him echoed the movement, an ink blot of darkness, silently mirroring his gestures. Becky watched the surreal display, unable to keep her eyes away from the black shadow, hoping the cowl hiding the bent head would not move to reveal what it was covering.

Becky's eyes widened and she looked up through the glass to the Ops room where Hugh and Olly were watching anxiously. A glimpse of their faces told Becky that indeed she did not sound in control. Hugh shook his head at her, frowning, and half raised a hand in a thumbs-up sign, a gesture which through the glass looked more a question than an affirmation. She saw Hugh turn to Olly and say something. Olly shook his head and typed a message to Becky's computer screen.

Becky looked down and saw the message flash in front of her. 'Come on, Becky, have him!'

She gathered herself, focused her eyes on Bert and not the dark entity which seemed part of him. She knew that she was the only person seeing that dark form. She was alone in the studio with this thing, despite the presence in the next room of her production team and the audience tuned in worldwide. She swallowed, ignoring her dry mouth, and resumed her broadcast with a certainty she did not feel but manufactured with skill.

'Ah, the unicorn, at the centre of your astral enchantment ministry. When did the unicorns first appear to you?'

'We ride the stars,' said Bert. 'We play in the universe. We harness the Astral Enchantment and ride the cosmic wave!'

'Quite. But what does that mean, exactly?' asked Becky. 'And if you work with a unicorn… is that a mythical symbol of your so-called healing powers or an actual horse with a horn on its head?'

Bert's eyes narrowed and the muscles in his neck moved dangerously. 'You may be an unbeliever, you with your nice little act of talking to the dead,' Bert's voice lost its acquired timbre and climbed up two octaves, riding the steroid wave, 'but I can make the lame walk, I can take away tumours, and I have the *POWER OF THE UNICORN!*'

Becky felt almost pushed back in her seat by the volume and anger coming from Brookings as he shouted at her. She heard a click in her headphones and Hugh's voice on talkback, sniggering in her ear. 'He needs to calm down, Becky, but Olly says let him rock.' Becky suddenly felt less isolated, more in control, and she knew just what to do next.

She nodded towards Olly and Hugh in Ops.

Becky paused, her silence deliberate this time, just to make sure that Bert's loss of control was clearly emphasised. Her voice was now calm and steady. 'Yes, the power of the unicorn. I am just interested – as many of your followers do believe in astral enchantment – in where this first came to you. And where you believe your ability to – how shall I put it? – oh yes, that power to heal comes from?'

Bert's mouth opened and closed like a goldfish. The black entity with Bert seemed to be growing in height slightly. She was sure the black space was taller, wider – only slightly, but she was sure there was a change. She shifted her gaze back to Brookings, whose fists were clenching and unclenching.

'My power is from a place you can't even begin to imagine, girl.' Bert spoke slowly; he leaned forward, staring Becky right in the eyes. 'We ride the stars, we touch the Astral Enchantment, and the Power of the Unicorn guides us. If you had half a brain cell, which you clearly don't, for all the la di da coming out of your gob, you wouldn't dare to question my power. You, with your own radio show, your fancy black frock and that tame queen of yours.' Brookings jabbed his fist in the direction of Hugh Jolly, watching wide-eyed in Ops. 'Don't you condescend to me, you bloody ginger who once went to bloody Cambridge.' Becky leaned even further back in her chair, her eyes flicking from Bert to the black mass attached to him as she fought the urge to get up and run out of the studio.

Bert slammed his fist down on the felt-covered table, making her jump. 'My healing energy comes from out there, the stars, the frikin' cosmos. And with my touch, I heal the sick, the weary, and the faithful!'

The mention of the vulnerable, whom Becky knew Brookings was exploiting, brought her a measure of steady anger. She pushed her fear aside and knew she had to expose this ranting charlatan once and for all.

'How do you respond to the medical community here in Britain, who are sceptical about your claims to heal?' Becky was very calm, but her eyes flicked from Bert to the black entity behind him.

'What do they know?' shouted Bert. 'I take what their drugs and their machines and their radiation cannot begin to touch, and I *make it go away*! My hands heal. I *am* the healer! It's the *Power of the Unicorn*!'

'And yet,' said Becky, forcing her voice to be quiet and calm, 'the British Medical Association has disputed your healing claims. They say that abandoning conventional therapy and putting trust in a healer such as you is unethical and dangerous. Are you medically qualified?'

'My energy, my gift is here, girl.' Bert flexed his fingers towards Becky. 'These hands, these healing hands! Ask the thousands who come to me and throw away their crutches, throw away the morphine, who walk and see and who worship the Unicorn. They come to me when those quacks fail them. They come to me for the starlight. They come to me, they feel the love, they worship the Astral Enchantment and we *ride the astral plane*!' The voice rose another octave, and Becky pulled back again, this time at Bert's fingers waggling in her face.

'But what proof, apart from the faith of those who follow you, do you have that you can heal?'

'Have you seen my channel on YouTube? There are hundreds of testimonials on there. Many of the healed will be listening now. Love from the Unicorn!' Bert punched the air again, the black shadow, definitely larger, moving in perfect synchronicity. 'You unbelievers.' Bert sneered the word out, his Welsh accent getting more and more pronounced. 'You unbelievers, with your fancy stage shows and your fancy ways of talking, you will never feel the Power of the Unicorn!'

'So yes, this unicorn, did it just appear to you one day?' Becky asked. Bert smiled unpleasantly.

'The way was shown to me. On the astral plane, a symbol of healing power. We ride the enchantment plane, we share the power.' He appeared calmer now, and the black entity seemed to be smaller. 'Love is at the centre of everything. And I was created to bring love to the universe.'

'More, er, love from Bert Brookings and more astral enchantment on *Medium Wave*, next.'

Olly hit the commercial break. The *On Air* light clicked off; the microphones were muted. Brookings pointed his finger at Becky.

'You won't get me, you bitch.'

'Being angry and aggressive isn't doing you any favours, Bert,' Becky replied coolly. 'Call me a bitch again and I will make sure you crawl out of this studio with no reputation whatsoever. Your choice.'

Olly buzzed. 'Five seconds, doing great, Becky.'

It only took five seconds for Bert's anger to build again. Meanwhile, Becky was grimly fascinated by how the carbonised attachment reflected his mood. Brookings clearly had no idea that this thing was welded to his physical body.

'Welcome back to *Medium Wave* on The Voice of Britain. We are with the healer, Bert Brookings. Bert, have you always claimed to be able to heal?'

'It's not a claim!' he shouted.

'When did you first heal someone, then?' asked Becky, very calmly.

'I had been riding the cosmos, playing on the stars,' Bert said, as if this was an answer. Becky could see Hugh laughing and Olly suppressing a grin through the glass. Bert must also have seen them. His temper grew. 'All right, I laid my hands on a child.'

Becky's eyebrows rose. 'A child?'

'I know what you're thinking!' screamed Bert. 'You with your filthy minds, you *perverts*!'

Becky noticed as Nick frantically adjusted the microphone levels. She sighed. She may have been frightened by the black entity attached to this pugnacious, tattooed Welshman, but she was also weary of Bert's tantrum.

'Mr Brookings,' she said, 'I would appreciate it if you could calm down and answer the questions. Many of your followers are listening to *Medium Wave* right now and would like to know about your philosophy and about the unicorn. Shouting isn't the way. After all, don't you say love is the answer?'

Becky watched Brookings as he tensed, the muscles under the tight shirt rippling. She knew she was sitting opposite a man fighting a losing battle with his temper and she recoiled at the look of pure hatred on his face. Then she watched the carbon mass begin to expand.

'Oh, we all know about you, Becky Moran.' Bert's anger was making the muscles on his neck pulse with his heartbeat. 'You're a fake, you pretend to talk to the dead, but it's all *stage managed*!' he shouted. The density of the black entity grew deeper, darker. 'You swan about, you stuck-up bitch, taking good money from innocent people, cashing in on their grief and making mourning like an entertainment. If you had half the gift I have, they would burn you at the stake, you witch.'

Becky heard a click in her ear and Olly's voice telling her quite distinctly to 'wind this up, Becky, end this now. Calling Security.' Olly sounded frightened and she could see Hugh moving to the door of Ops.

Becky looked back at the raving Welshman. What he said didn't bother her, she could and would deal with that. Her eyes moved to the space behind him and became fixed on the dark appendage, bound by unseen threads to this angry man. As he accused her of being a fake, she saw with shock that the head, draped by the cowl, had begun to lift. As Bert Brookings suggested she should be burned as a witch, the head of the entity, this dark acolyte, was upright and the cowl started to fall backwards. Becky's feeling of fear intensified. There was a shift in the internal density, a darkness that was new.

'The world needs to know that you, the sainted bitch Becky Moran, are nothing but a sideshow, a fairground act. *A fake!*' Bert was screaming now, his voice high, the power of his muscular body straining against the tight t-shirt.

Becky, her eyes not leaving the blackness, said, 'Ladies and gentlemen, our apologies for the use of bad language by Mr Brookings. He is clearly unwell.' Brookings began to rise to his feet. 'Sit down,' she ordered. 'You need to be aware that standing right behind you is something very dark, something quite malevolent and, what's more, the entity seems connected to your emotions. I saw it the minute you came in. I have no idea what it is, but if I were you, Bert, I would get that thing under control right now or it will absorb you. I would say it comes from Hell.'

Bert twisted to look behind him, the now huge carbon shadow perfectly echoing his physical movement, and then his anger totally overtook him. He looked at Becky and grunted as he reached forward to grab hold of her, just as the studio door burst open and Hugh Jolly, hair flopping, ran over to tackle him, unaware that he was passing right through the dense black shape.

Becky pushed herself back in her chair, her headphones ripping off, to get away from Bert's lunge. She watched the towering blackness, now upright as the cowl slid away from a featureless, flat, blind disc. No eyes, thought Becky, no eyes, just a plateau of grey, a flat space where a face should have been. She heard a high-pitched howling, almost a shriek of rage and violence, the sound coming from the black depths. There was no doubt that the blackness wanted to absorb Brookings. It was Brookings. That grey space, that disc of opaque density, exuded hatred, pulsed with it, and she sensed, if not saw, just how twisted in rage it was.

Hugh was struggling to pin back Bert's arms; it wasn't easy, given his pumped-up muscular strength. Becky leant towards her microphone, fumbling for her headphones.

'We are trying to restrain Mr Brookings, and Security are on their way.' She was just a little flustered. 'Again, we can only apologise for this unexpected outburst from Mr Brookings.' The *On Air* light clicked off as Olly ordered an ad break and ran into the studio to help Hugh.

Bert Brookings was straining to attack Becky. The blackness was now touching him, and she wanted Hugh out of the way. She was certain that if the entity absorbed itself into Bert, like a cancerous amoeba, Hugh would dissolve into the darkness too. Olly reached them and took hold of Bert as a security guard ran into the studio. The three men managed to drag Bert away from the microphone and away from the desk, and the guard got him face down on the floor while Hugh and Olly held his arms behind his back. The guard fumbled for his cuffs.

The darkness, the shape, the blot of blackness began to shrink, the cowl draping back over the grey disc, that space that was not a face. The blot bent over again as Bert Brookings was restrained on the floor. He did not struggle; it was as if all the energy had drained out of him.

Outside, the lights of police cars illuminated the Cube, casting their intermittent blue flashes into the studio, hitting the walls and bouncing off the glass frontage

Becky sat back down at her microphone as the police escorted Brookings, his arms restrained behind his back, out of the studio. As he was walked out, head down, the black ink blot of a shape moved silently behind him, unseen by everyone but herself. Becky wanted that thing and Brookings out of her sight. Hugh swept back his hair and caught his breath. Becky watched Sarah snapping pictures on her iPhone. 'I have all of it, Hugh,' she said, and then walked over to Becky, her earrings clanking as she looked at Becky with concern. 'The nutter has gone, Becky – are you okay?' Becky nodded and briefly held Sarah's hand, taking comfort from her friend's concern. Sarah squeezed her hand.

Becky looked at Olly, who was standing in front of her. He looked pale and shaken.

'Can you carry on, Becky?' he asked.

'Yes,' she said. Sarah, Hugh and Olly went back into Ops and the red light clicked on. 'Well, an eventful few minutes here at The Voice of Britain,' she said, 'but Mr Brookings is now in police custody and I can assure you I am unharmed. We wish him well as it appears he was not what we have to assume is his normal self. Ladies and gentlemen, as you know, I can see and speak to spirits and I want to share with you that I did see a form, an entity if you will, near to Bert Brookings. I must also tell you I have no idea what it was. It did not speak to me. I know many of you who follow the unicorn will be concerned about Mr Brookings's behaviour, and any further statement about him will come from the Metropolitan Police in due course.

'I am Becky Moran and *Medium Wave* will return next Friday at eight. From the team here at The Voice of Britain, have a good weekend and may the spirits be kind until we meet again.'

Nick hit the jingle that ended the show and the red light clicked off.

Aiden O'Conner had finished his chat with John X and made his way down to the ground floor just in time to see the police taking some bodybuilder-type out through Reception, the blue lights of the police car sweeping through the glass walls of the Cube. He thundered his way into the Ops room, where Olly was taking calls and reassuring listeners that Becky was indeed all right. Hugh was talking on his mobile to the *Daily Mail*, who apparently wanted to see if he had any pictures and were asking if Becky would give them an exclusive interview. Sarah was sitting in the studio with Becky.

'What the fuck went on this time?' roared O'Conner. Sarah stood up as Hugh motioned for her to deal with Aiden.

'Bert Brookings went loco on air. He swore and went for Becky. Had these two not restrained him, he would have attacked her,' she said. O'Conner did a quick mental calculation as to whether this was good or bad for ratings, decided it was good – listening back to the interview would confirm later that Becky had been exemplary and in fact could win an award for how she handled it – and so nodded at Becky Moran, cool as ever, with her shoes still discarded next to her and her red hair unruffled. Becky nodded back. O'Conner left to listen back to the last part of *Medium Wave* and to prepare a statement for the press.

Every phone line into the studio was flashing. Trending on social media was a picture of Brookings, tweeted by Sarah, showing Bert prostrate on the floor of the studio, his face clearly visible with one cheek squashed flat and his hands cuffed behind his back. The tagline was @MediumWave #Unicornfloored! Sarah told Hugh she hoped that picture would make the front pages of all the tabloids on Saturday morning.

Becky's exclusive with the *Daily Mail* the next day included a photograph, etched in black and white, her speaking of her sympathy for Bert, and highlighted her very special gift. It was a very sympathetic article, with the headline 'Medium Waves Off Unicorn!'

'Of course, we shall press charges,' Hugh was saying, as he topped up his glass of vodka with ice in the Soho Club an hour after they had left the Cube. The team had met the paparazzi as they left the studios and Becky had posed solemnly for the cameras but declined to comment.

'Oh, he's unhinged. Let him just spend a night in the cells,' said Becky. 'He didn't hurt me.'

'He would have,' said Sarah, gulping a very large gin sling. 'It took all of them to pin him down.'

Hugh sipped his liquor. 'Well, his astral bollocks and love talk will be dead in a dustbin now.' He was clearly pleased that the publicity was not going to harm Divine Diva at all. 'But what did you see, that thing behind Bert?' he asked. Olly sighed at the question. Dealing with a nutter who believed in unicorns and belting women was one thing, but to have the sophisticated and urbane Hugh Jolly lapping up this psychic crap was just unbelievable.

'I don't know,' said Becky. 'I haven't seen anything like it before. Though to be honest, I've seen so much this last week, I'm beginning to think that nothing could surprise me anymore.' She picked up her glass of red wine, looking from Olly to Hugh and Sarah. 'Here's to dead unicorns and to us. Thanks, guys, for saving me.'

Olly raised his glass and clinked it against Becky's.

CHAPTER ELEVEN

Becky was standing outside one of her favourite London bookshops, Watkins Books in Cecil Court, tucked away just off the Charing Cross Road in the West End. Bookshops of any description were places where Becky had always found peace, whether it was Waterstones in Leeds or any second-hand bookshop she might wander into. Cambridge was full of them. The smell of the books, that magical dry smell, the colours of the covers, the words running within the pages, the wisdom and knowledge, the stories. Lifting the actual book and turning the pages, letting someone else tell their story; Becky loved it. In a world of download and discard, an actual book was forever.

Watkins was one of those rare bookshop finds. It was different. The Victorian-style glass windows edged in black and gold always reminded Becky of an old-fashioned apothecary. Instead of glass bottles filled with potions gleaming with jewel colours, or scattered, decorated boxes of salves and jars filled with pills and perfume, the contents of Watkins were even more esoteric. The shop was old, almost rickety inside. Staircases with wooden bannisters led you up to half floors and down, twisting, into the cellar. Specialising in Mind, Body and Spirit, you could find books on magic, the occult, and every brand of spirituality going. Pictures of the Dalai Lama were propped up against books of ancient spells. Tables were sprawled with supernatural offerings, religious texts, and philosophical guidance. There were four wide glass windows looking out onto Cecil Court and a heavy door that you had to push to open. Becky always thought this was a symbol: there should be no easy entry to a place filled with so many different belief systems.

It was Monday and Becky had a couple of hours to spare before she got the train up to Leeds. The *Medium Wave* team had had their weekly production meeting at the Cube that morning. Sarah now had two days of one-on-one mediumship readings planned for Becky, which she would do at the flat, in the attic of a converted Methodist chapel in Leeds. Sarah had handed over the research notes, saying shyly that she didn't think Becky would need them any more. Becky said best to take them, to be sure, and thanked her.

Olly would be meeting her later in the week, once he had confirmed the start of filming for the TV pilot. He was going to book a crew to recce a film location in what was supposed to be a haunted Lancaster bomber from World War II, now a museum piece. Becky had made it clear she wasn't going to film anything that so many others sensationalised and bad TV series did time and again, with night vision photography so that everyone had silver eyes and with hysterical mediums scaring the cameramen. Olly had assured her that this so-called haunting was 'bloody fascinating' and would make great TV; no one had ever filmed there, despite the reports of ghostly activity. He would call and brief her fully later.

O'Conner had burst his way into their meeting, stomach first, the buttons straining seriously around his navel. He had spent the weekend on a freebie at Belmond le Manoir aux Quat'Saisons in Oxfordshire as a guest of Raymond Blanc and had stuffed down so much foie gras that, if he were to be squeezed, it would regurgitate out of him like a grey ribbon of bile. He'd stood at the back of the meeting, saying nothing but oozing intimidation. He looked at Becky constantly. Sarah had told Becky later that she wanted to punch his lights out. When they'd finished their meeting, he said, 'Friday went well. More wackjobs, please, Olly,' and left the room.

Becky was not after a book at Watkins this afternoon. She knew there almost certainly wasn't one to explain what she was experiencing. No, it was the cabinets filled with charms and candles and jewellery and dream catchers she wanted to see. You could buy anything from a Native American necklace to a Goth-style ring in the shape of a skull; Becky smiled when she saw those, remembering sweating Henry and the brick shithouse. She just wanted something to wear to protect her. Never one for jewellery, she nevertheless rationalised that any protection against the dark was better than nothing.

She explained what she wanted to the girl at Watkins, who was wearing so much ornate silver jewellery that Becky couldn't help thinking that were she to go through airport security the scanner would explode. The girl was a listener to *Medium Wave*.

'That unicorn bloke was well out of order, Becky.' She picked out some charms that were supposed to protect the wearer from harm. 'What you need is an amulet,' she said, and her fingers, cluttered heavily with silver rings, laid out a series of small charms. What caught Becky's attention first was a small turquoise amulet, a disc edged with filigree silver on a delicate chain. 'A very nice one, that,' said the girl. 'It's beautiful. But, well, I hope you don't mind me saying, Ms Moran... you see, its main property is boosting psychic communication. And I don't think you need that, do you? How about...' She indicated a snowflake obsidian crystal amulet in a half-moon shape. The stone was coal black with white flecks and felt warm to the touch. 'I mean, you couldn't belt that Brookings with it, but the powers of protection with this stone and the shape are well known.' Becky nodded and slipped it around her neck. It felt good. She could tuck it inside her trademark dress when she was on stage or working, and for now, it sat perfectly against the crisp white shirt she was wearing, topped off by an expensive biker-style leather jacket over black skinny jeans and shiny flat brogues. Until recently, Becky would have scoffed at the idea of wearing a good-luck charm, never mind an amulet. Now, she felt she needed all the help she could get.

Bert Brookings was not charged with attempted assault because Becky did not want to press charges. Hugh Jolly went ballistic, saying the lunatic needed a criminal record and, moreover, he needed locking up. Becky just told Hugh he wasn't worth the bother. The Voice of Britain had lost a major advertiser but that wouldn't be a problem as there were enough peddlers of the esoteric out there who wanted to sell their wares, especially as the ratings were so good.

Hugh had heard that many of the Unicorn faithful had been outraged at the way Bert had lost his temper; one American group of followers had even posted warnings on the Internet over the weekend that Bert Brookings was a man of violence and a fake. The picture of him handcuffed on the floor was reproduced, framed in a red box as if to emphasise how dangerous he was. They also posted a picture of Brookings being restrained by Hugh and Olly. The weekend revenue stream for Astral Enchantment was down dramatically and Brookings returned to his Welsh farm with any credibility he'd had going the way of his penis: shrinking. No one had seen or heard from him since the police let him go late on Friday night with a warning and a suggestion that he needed anger management. Even the *Daily Star* couldn't get through.

Becky's fame was growing, however. After the studio ruck on Friday, the exclusive in the *Daily Mail* and the Internet chatter, the shares on Twitter and Facebook streams, Hugh saw with pleasure that the show at the Dominion Theatre next Sunday was now a sell-out. The tech team were blogging on Becky's behalf and online sales and subscriptions were up. Hugh was getting requests for Becky to do interview slots on daytime TV and he'd taken a call late on Sunday night from the organiser of a major supernatural festival in Las Vegas who wanted Becky to do a guest slot. And Olly was shaping the TV pilot very nicely, despite the disappointment of that mirror in York.

Hugh thought he may get some flavoured vodka in to celebrate. That and the very nice young man he had his eye on at the Soho Club.

Becky arrived at the flat in Leeds by mid-evening. Her mother had popped in earlier with bleach ('In case you need it, love') and had put fresh milk in the fridge. She opened the front door to the flat, looking at the white sofa, the French décor, and smiled. The huge windows let in the glow of the streetlights. Becky snapped on all the electric lights using the switch by the door and, for the first time in over a week, she felt at home. She had caught a cab from the Leeds City station, picking up some food from the Marks and Spencer located by the main entrance. She had seen many spirits on the streets of London and on the train north, and also seen a group of them in City Square in Leeds, gathered around the statue of the Black Prince on his horse. None of the spirits bothered her. Becky had been visualising her own protective white aura. What with that and the amulet, she felt she was starting to take control of whatever was happening to her.

Then, something caught her eye, by the sofa.

It looked at first glance like a piece of lace, a thick black ribbon. No, the corner of a silk lace scarf. She could just see the edge of the fine cloth. She knew it wasn't hers and very much doubted that it belonged to Iris. ('Black is so ageing, Becky. Wear colour, especially with that hair,' was a mantra she'd heard her mother repeat so often.) Becky stepped into the room. The light did not change and there was no bad smell creeping into her nose. She put the bags down and closed the front door.

Becky edged cautiously towards the sofa, bending from the waist to examine the cloth. It moved, as if wafted on a slight breeze, and Becky jumped back. There were no draughts in the room. She moved closer again and could see that the cloth was almost iridescent, not black, more a shimmering dark red, and she knew she was seeing something from the Other Side, not woven of Earthly fibres, not real or solid or of this world. As she reached the back of the sofa, the ethereal fabric was revealed to be a long swathe of twisted red cloth, laid out at the edge of the sofa. The fronds at the end of the unearthly rope lay in a perfect fan on the floor, as if placed there gently. They were frayed and delicate. Becky stared at the shape, wondering how a fine fabric could be bound together and twisted into a solid rope.

Becky's eyes followed the line of the cloth. She was waiting for that terrible blackness to come rushing at her, for the thrum, thrum, thrum to begin. She tensed, preparing to flee. There was silence.

The end of the rope was wrapped and knotted around the neck of a woman. She was lying on the floor, coiled into a foetal shape, her once blonde hair swept back, exposing a young face that appeared to be sleeping. Becky was afraid, but it was a different fear. She knew this was a spirit. She traced the path of the cloth right around the neck of the woman who wasn't really there yet lay curled on the floor. There was a sense of overwhelming sadness and pain that Becky could feel in her gut. The rope had dug deep into the neck and Becky could see the marks on the unearthly flesh, blue and mottled, of the exposed throat. She was dressed in what looked like a long white cotton nightdress, the material resting over the curves of her limbs. She simply lay there, the extraordinary red rope in shocking contrast to the paleness of this being. There was no movement.

Until the woman opened her eyes.

Becky took a step back. The spirit looked at her with such longing, such agony, and her hands, the not-quite-real hands, clawed at the rope around her neck. In the silence, Becky heard the wordless pleading of this girl to help her, to save her.

'I can't,' whispered Becky. 'I can't.' Becky understood – no, felt – that the life of this young woman had ended here, in what was once the attic of this Methodist chapel. She also knew that this girl had taken her own life, using the twisted red scarf to hang herself from one of the beams overhead. Becky felt her desperation, depression, sadness; it was almost overwhelming. There was no malice, no evil, and no threat here, just a yearning for the pain to end. Becky realised that the spirit had never left this attic. She'd always been here, like a faint photograph, stuck in the place where her life had ended. Becky's fear was replaced by compassion.

'You can go,' she whispered. 'I can see you and you can go. It's all right, you have suffered too long. Time to let go, move on.' The pale figure, bound by that shimmering red, twisted scarf, seemed to quieten. The hands left her neck where she had been so desperately trying to unbind the red rope and slowly, very slowly, her body began to fade. 'You can go,' Becky repeated softly.

As she looked down, the girl, the spirit, was dissolved almost into nothingness, her eyes finally closed. The final glimpse, the last thing to fade, was that shimmering red rope, until nothing remained.

Early on Thursday morning, Olly picked Becky up from Grimsby railway station and they headed out in his battered old Land Rover, over the flatlands to a small, privately owned museum on the site of what had once been RAF Grimsby – known as Waltham by its men – during the Second World War. A TV crew were on their way and would meet Olly and Becky at ten o'clock.

Olly gave Becky some background on the way. Known locally as 'the Aeroplane Graveyard', the museum was set in a restored hangar on farmland that had once been a bomber station. Abandoned after the war, one enthusiast had gathered a small collection of now-defunct aircraft and restored them to their former glory. James Cantrell, ex-RAF, had a Spitfire, two Mosquitos, and even a Messerschmitt. None of these aircraft was airworthy but nonetheless were magnificent. The pride of his collection was a fully restored Lancaster bomber. It had pride of place in the huge hangar where the exhibits of former warfare now sat out the post-war years. For Cantrell, it was a way of preserving history, and tourists and aircraft enthusiasts flocked to see these legendary warriors of the sky in their final resting place. It had taken years and a great deal of money to collect and restore these flying machines. Cantrell had been able to buy part of the disused Lincolnshire airfield for a song.

During the Second World War, Waltham had been a heavy bomber station with three different squadrons stationed there, attacking targets across Germany and the occupied countries of Europe. It had closed in 1945, was used by the RAF for maintenance work for a while and was then abandoned. A memorial to the 100 Squadron of Lancasters stood near the hangar.

'Locals claim they see ghosts there all the time,' Olly was explaining to Becky as they took a turning down a minor road off the A16 signed Waltham Aircraft Museum. 'Ghosts of airmen out in the fields. One woman swears she saw an RAF flyer walk through her wardrobe one night. Her house is on the edge of the airfield.'

Becky looked out of the window of the Land Rover, over the Lincolnshire countryside framed in the late September light. It was a misty morning, cold, an autumn chill in the air. The sunlight was watery, the colours of fading summer texturising the arable farmland. As Olly drove, she knew it wasn't the local legends of airmen ghosts they were after: it was the Lancaster bomber.

'The whole place is haunted, so says Cantrell.' Olly changed down a gear to second as the road became bumpy. 'He claims you can hear the bombing raids taking place and see the airmen. No one will stay in that hangar after dark. It may be a bit of great publicity-seeking, but he doesn't need it. These aircraft attract visitors from all over the world. Cantrell says this relic is actually frightening but he's asked you to take a look.'

Becky wanted an assurance that they were not going to do the hysterical medium-hears-things-go-bump-on-a-plane act. Olly said, 'Nah, of course not. This isn't any more haunted than your local Tesco, but the plane is magnificent, and the pictures will be amazing. You just do what you do. You know Hugh, he thinks it's a great piece for the pilot show – Cambridge medium does "Doors to Manual and Crosscheck", camping it up like you work for EasyJet. You point out the emergency exits, say "This is Medium Wave Airlines, next stop the pit of Hell"...' Olly started to laugh then stopped when Becky looked at him.

'Knock it off, Olly,' she said. 'You have no idea.'

The last two days had been interesting for Becky. Once that pale figure with the shining red, twisted rope around her neck had faded to nothingness, Becky had felt drained. She'd sat down on the plump white sofa and gathered herself. She sensed nothing evil in the flat, but knew she had two days ahead of readings for eight clients, all wanting to hear directly from the dead.

She had begun to realise this 'gift' she had acquired was powerful. Whilst she saw so much that was benign and clearly there (if not quite), she knew there was something else in those other dimensions that was hungry and waiting for her. In a world of the totally unknown, Becky realised how vulnerable she was. She slept, dreaming of that white light. By day, for each client she'd seen, the spirits had been there waiting to come through. Some of them even came through early, way before their loved one arrived at the flat in Leeds, and Becky had to control their presence and mentally tell them to come back later. She felt like a teacher in an infants' school, telling the spirits to line up and await their turn. It worked. Spirits seemed nothing if not patient.

Nothing else to do but wait, thought Becky, wryly.

She had done her research on the bomber. Cantrell had rescued it, extremely damaged, from the site near Aylesby, just to the north, where it had crashed when returning to Waltham from a raid over Normandy on a cloudy July day in 1943. Four of the seven crewmen had been killed. Just over seven thousand Lancasters were built during World War II and ND413 was one of only seventeen that were now intact and restored, housed in museums. Cantrell had excavated the site, removed what was left in sections, and spent years with a team of experts renovating it. Visitors could go inside, sit in the cockpit, climb to the upper or rear gun turrets, and even handle a Browning 0.303 machine gun. This Lancaster would never fly again, however, as the Rolls Royce Merlin engines were long gone. But it was the nearest anyone could get to experiencing what the airmen endured in those dangerous bombing raids.

Becky was not wearing her heels today but was dressed in a flowing black coat from a small boutique in the Victoria Quarter of Leeds. It was in keeping with her image, with just a touch of the theatrical. Her amulet was tucked safely under the thin woollen sweater she was wearing.

Olly pulled the Land Rover to a halt outside a small collection of buildings, dwarfed by the entrance to a giant aircraft hangar. 'Waltham Aircraft Museum' was printed in huge letters over the hangar door.

The hangar was positioned at the edge of the airfield. Now mainly agricultural land, most of the original buildings had disappeared. The control tower still stood at the end of what remained of the runway. Becky looked over the flatlands to the outline of the runway, overgrown with grass like a forgotten highway. She could see what looked like a golf course in the distance and another, smaller hangar. It was not difficult to imagine this place during the war. All that was missing were the bombers, parked and ready to scramble, with Vera Lynn blasting out from the speakers. In many ways, it was as if time had stood still here.

Becky looked towards the giant hangar in front of the Land Rover. A sprightly man in his late sixties, hair cut in a short back and sides and with a military bearing, was talking to the camera crew who had already arrived to set up their equipment and were now walking around the buildings.

'That's Cantrell,' said Olly, who had been up here on a recce with the crew earlier in the week.

'Do we salute?' asked Becky, smiling.

Cantrell had sharp eyes and clearly quite an eye for Becky. She saw him watch her climb out of the Land Rover with Olly, and he looked at her with approval. He listened to her Voice of Britain show on a Friday night and he'd told Olly that was why he wanted her to come and take a look at what was going on here. He smiled and extended his hand in welcome. Becky was reminded of the actor Leslie Phillips and half-expected him to say, 'Well, hellooooo,' when he spoke to her. Cantrell was dressed like a country squire in immaculately pressed chinos and polo-necked jumper, his windbreaker jacket a reminder of the morning's chill. He was unfailingly polite and clearly delighted to invite Becky and the film crew to his museum.

Olly had already briefed Becky. Cantrell was from a military family and his connection to the Lancaster was an emotional one. His uncle, Raymond Newport, had been a Lancaster bomber squadron leader, decorated for his bravery. Pictures of him taken during the war showed a handsome, charming man, squinting at the sunlight with his crew at his side, proudly showing off their aircraft. He was killed over Germany in 1942, leaving a pregnant wife. He had been just twenty-six. What inspired James Cantrell was more than a love of military aircraft: this was a family homage to a young man who had been a war hero and flown 'The Lanc'. The need to preserve history and remember Raymond was what drove Cantrell. The fact that there was something very, very wrong now that the restored bomber was in place was causing this usually pragmatic and decent man to doubt his own sanity.

Olly had met Cantrell earlier in the week and was looking forward to seeing the aircraft once more. Becky got ready to start filming as Olly ran through the final checks and schedule with the film crew.

'Do you scare easily, Miss Moran?' Cantrell asked as the sound technician, Brendon, was attaching her lapel mic and fixing the battery unit onto the waistband of her black skinny jeans.

'Sometimes,' replied Becky honestly. 'Should I be scared now?'

Cantrell shook his head and gestured that Becky should step inside the hangar. 'We shall see, shan't we?'

CHAPTER TWELVE

Becky Moran stepped inside the huge, dark hangar, her eyes trying to adjust to the contrast after the bright sunlight outside in that flat Lincolnshire field. She was now absorbed into the almost inky darkness. It made her blink. She was inside a huge, cavernous space, windowless, with a high vaulted roof, that looked like a modern cathedral of war. No altar here, just the dark, almost menacing shapes of the aircraft. The smaller planes circled one enormous black silhouette: the Lancaster bomber, centre stage.

Cantrell nodded to a member of staff to switch on the spotlights that illuminated the exhibits. They beamed out almost like searchlights, the type she had seen from images of the war, lights that swung in arcs up into the night sky, trying to spot enemy aircraft. The hangar was revealed. Other ground lights shone up at the metal fuselages, highlighting the paintwork and gleaming metal. The nose of the Lancaster, with that iconic bulbous Perspex cupola cockpit, stared back at Becky and Cantrell as Olly joined them through the hangar door.

'It is magnificent,' Olly said to Cantrell, nodding towards the bomber.

'Thank you. It took decades to restore. We had to hunt down most of the parts and we used an aviation expert to be absolutely accurate. All these,' he gestured towards his collection, 'are the result of much love and effort.'

'Why did you do it?' asked Becky.

Cantrell repeated the story of his uncle, the squadron leader. 'It is our history, my history, a tribute to the men and women who built them and especially to the men who flew them. Without having them here, as they once were, history would forget. We should not forget their sacrifice, ever, Miss Moran.'

The chief cameraman, Steve, came into the hangar. Tall and blond, he wore jeans and a dark blue sweatshirt that clung over a slight beer belly, testament to his love of real ale. He carried a large digital camera. Olly already had the shoot mapped out.

Becky would do an introduction outside, moving inside the hangar to chat to Cantrell about the museum and what he claimed was going on in the Lancaster; then, this evening, when it was dark, Cantrell, Becky, and Steve, with the sound technician moving with them, would climb inside it.

Becky looked around the hangar at the exhibition panels that decorated the walls, illustrating each aircraft in flight and with text giving a history of their manufacture and deployment in war. A huge Union flag hung over one wall to remind visitors who indeed had won the war. There was no Nazi flag near the Messerschmitt, but that aircraft also had information about its own technological history, giving the visitor an idea of Luftwaffe airpower.

Becky found all the aircraft somehow sinister, their shapes reminding her of huge black moths of death. There was no payload on the Lancaster, but she still sensed the power of this carrier of destruction. This aircraft had been the most successful night-time bomber of World War II. She looked along its unique shape, taking in the two elliptical upright fins at the rear and the turrets where gunners would fire from the nose, from the raised mid-section and at the rear over the tail. The long, deep belly of this beast had carried many thousands of tons of bombs over great distances, and later modified to take Barnes Wallis's famous Upkeep bouncing bombs for the attacks on the Ruhr Valley dams.

She shuddered. But, for once, it wasn't her supernatural ability that was in charge here, just a reaction to the toys of war. Olly, she could see, loved it. She wouldn't have been surprised if he'd started running about with his arms outstretched, pretending to bomb Jerry, and making rat-a-tat-tat noises. All he'd need was an RAF uniform and he would be shouting 'Chocks away!' and regressing to the age of eight. Inwardly, Becky rolled her eyes.

They filmed Becky's introduction outside the hangar. Before the camera rolled, she touched up her make-up and brushed her hair. She was aware of Cantrell watching her closely, clearly impressed.

'This is Waltham Aircraft Museum in Lincolnshire.' Becky spoke to the camera, a slight breeze just fluffing her long, red hair. 'Inside this hangar lie some of the most important aircraft of the Second World War, including a Spitfire that fought in the Battle of Britain and two small, fast Mosquito bombers. But it is the fully restored, huge Lancaster bomber that I have come to see. An aircraft said to be haunted by the crew who once flew missions over war-torn Europe before it crashed just north of here, killing four of the seven crewmen on board, two years before the war ended. I am told that no one will stay in this hangar after dark.

'But I shall…'

'Cut!' shouted Olly, asking Becky to record that one more time, just for good measure. He had told her he'd already worked out his use of archive film of a Lancaster in action together with some stills of the renovation and how he would cut all that into Becky's narrative. 'The Cambridge Medium' for television had well and truly begun.

Next, Becky was to interview Cantrell. Inside the hangar, Olly had set up two chairs underneath the nose of the bomber, beautifully framing the arc of its wing where the now-defunct Rolls Royce Merlin engines were housed. The camera shot included the museum background. There were two cameras so that Steve could cut into Becky's face and film Cantrell at the same time. The crew were arranging the set-up as Becky walked back into the hangar. She sat in her chair while the technician adjusted the lights. Cantrell came and sat opposite her, and they waited for Steve to position them. Becky looked up at the huge bomber behind them.

'What have you experienced in there?' she asked.

'I've never been so afraid,' said Cantrell, 'and I don't scare easily. It started when we finally wheeled her into the hangar and began to prepare her for display. There were two of us inside, late one evening about a year ago. I swear to you, Becky, the temperature dropped considerably, suddenly. We could feel a vibration and then…' Cantrell paused and looked down. 'I heard them.'

'Heard what?'

'The voices, screaming and shouting, and we saw—'

Olly stepped up, smiling. 'Ready?'

Becky nodded, smoothed her hair, and checked her lipstick was in place. Steve moved her chair slightly towards Cantrell, made him sit slightly forward, then checked the viewfinder on both. He put his thumbs up to Olly.

'And... go!' said Olly.

Becky looked to camera one and welcomed the viewer inside the hangar. Olly had explained there would be a long shot of the Lancaster and other planes in the museum to be cut into the film before her interview. She talked to Cantrell about the recovery of the Lancaster and what he knew of its history. Although the interview would be too long for broadcast, Olly would edit it down later. Unlike live radio, creating television was time-consuming. The set-up shots, camera detail, and construction of a piece for TV were complex. Becky thought she preferred the immediacy and intimacy of her live radio studio, but she was enjoying this experience.

She asked Cantrell why he thought this Lancaster bomber was haunted, what he had experienced. Again, Cantrell looked down and told the story of being inside the aircraft and hearing voices, the cold temperature, and a vibration within the plane.

'There is no working engine, no moving parts as such?' asked Becky.

'No, this is just a shell. But believe me, I do not for one minute think it is empty.'

'Cut!' yelled Olly. 'Lovely. Okay, we'll do some set-up shots now of you both going onto the plane. Then back this evening about five and we'll film in there when it's dark.'

Becky was enjoying a day without much spirit interference. This abandoned airfield was a bleak, beautiful space, but it was a relief to be away from crowds and clients and spirits with their messages. Nothing ever lingered around Olly. But Cantrell had his dead father and his uncle Raymond standing beside him, looking proud that their boy had taken the family military tradition to the next level. She told Cantrell. He was pleased if a bit spooked.

'Has my father any message for me?' Cantrell asked.

'No,' said Becky, 'but he is with you.'

'Never did say much, even when he was alive,' was Cantrell's weary answer.

They all piled off to the local pub for a late lunch. It would take a while for the camera crew to set up the lights and install the camera feed into the interior of the Lancaster where Becky and Cantrell would be filmed. Cantrell bought a round of drinks as the TV crew got stuck-in to their large plates of chicken and chips. Steve asked Becky to pass the vinegar.

'Are you really psychic?' he asked.

'Yes, I am,' she replied.

Olly gave her a slightly exasperated look. 'Just act it out tonight, Becky. Just give us a feeling of what it was like to fly the Lancaster. Spook it up. It'll be fine.'

'Olly thinks this is all hokum,' she said to Steve, smiling, 'but it makes great entertainment. Don't worry, Olly, I'm sure that if there's anything there, we can get it on film.'

'Nervous?' asked Olly, after a while. He would have meant because they were filming for the first time. Becky looked at him and remembered he didn't know anything about hags trapped in mirrors, dark apparitions coming at her from upstairs in her house in Cambridge, or suicide spirits haunting her flat in Leeds.

'Should I be?' she replied, with a smile.

It was a dark night with no moon – not even what they used to call a bomber's moon – outside the hangar in that Lincolnshire field.

Entry to the Lancaster was up a metal walkway with side rails. A door led into the main body of the plane. To the left was the pilot's cockpit and the narrow bomb aimer's position that doubled up with the two front guns; beside the pilot on a folding seat would be the flight engineer and immediately behind them would sit the navigator at a small metal table, using primitive instruments or even the stars to guide the mission; to the right and in the cramped fuselage above the long bomb bay, sat the radio operator. Small steps led to the upper turret that housed two more guns, while at the rear the highly exposed lookout and four-gun position for 'Tail End Charlie' could just be made out.

The technicians had rigged remote cameras at fixed points, with bright lights shining from every angle throughout the spartan interior of the aircraft. Ropes and straps hung from the inside of the fuselage and there was an immediate smell of gun oil and ageing metal. This hollow, metal tube that had helped Britain win the war was sparse and utilitarian, a bomb delivery machine.

Becky hated it the minute she walked in. It felt extremely claustrophobic, despite the size of this flying fortress. Steve was ahead of her, walking backwards with his camera on his shoulder to get the action shots as Cantrell walked just behind her. Inside the bomber, Becky described how she felt and what she could see while Cantrell pointed out the interior features. Steve had a headphone link to Olly, who was in the main exhibition space watching what was being filmed, streamed live onto a monitor positioned by the wheels of the aircraft. The sound recordist, Brendon, was just behind Cantrell, down on the floor and out of the sight of the camera angles, monitoring the sound levels.

Just as Cantrell was explaining how the navigator communicated to the pilot, Becky felt a slight vibration. She looked at Cantrell. Steve looked down at his feet, puzzled.

'Do you feel that?' asked Becky. Brendon gestured that he was picking up a vibration. Olly, through the remote link and hearing and feeling nothing out in the quiet hanger, told Steve to carry on filming.

Becky looked into the camera lens, outwardly calm. But her whole body was tense and a feeling of being shut in, oppressed, borne down upon, was steadily getting stronger. She stared into the camera, waiting for darkness to wrap itself around her. The scent of gun oil was strong, but that was all she could smell.

'There is a vibration,' Becky said, her voice shaking slightly. She put out her hand to the side of the aircraft to steady herself. She turned her head and caught sight of Cantrell behind her, his eyes wide, darting around the interior, his face ashen. Becky felt as if every one of her five senses was heightened. The temperature in the Lancaster was dropping rapidly and Becky's breath emerged as a ghostly grey plume as she spoke.

'Can you hear that, James?' she asked Cantrell, her eyes flicking along the fuselage. 'I can hear voices, the voices of men.'

Cantrell shook his head and stepped back.

'Shit,' Brendon muttered as Cantrell stumbled over him and out of the aircraft. Becky saw him leave and had a brief glimpse of him shaking his head, as if he was being urged to get back in;

his expression was one of fear mingled with shame as he was clearly refusing to do so.

She was now standing, feeling isolated, inside the Lancaster bomber, Steve and his camera in front of her. He was shaking, and Becky couldn't work out if it was fear or the bitter cold that surrounded them. He kept the camera aimed at Becky's face so she could see her pale reflection in the lens. 'Olly says we must keep on filming,' he told her, his voice uncertain. The camera shook slightly in his hands as Becky felt the vibration of the aircraft intensify. It became a roar and she put her hands up to her ears to try and block it out. Becky stood unsteadily in front of Steve, her face screwed up against a sound that to her was almost deafening.

She stepped back. Brendon was crouching somewhere at her feet as she pressed herself against the fuselage.

'I can see, I can see...' she said, her head turning towards the rear of the plane. She saw something move; her eyes were fixed, glistening. In her field of vision, the remote cameras and bright lights that the TV crew had fixed up had disappeared. She saw smoke swirling within the bomber and, emerging through it, the outline of an airman staggering towards her, his mouth open and screaming. His hair was on fire. She could smell it, that scorched horror, as he reached with arms outstretched towards her. He fell before he could touch her.

The reflection of Becky's face in the camera lens was twisted in fear and horror. Steve was still shaking, but it was clear he had not seen what she had, or he would have run out of the plane, she thought. Becky pressed her body against the fuselage, as if to meld with the metal and somehow dissolve her way out of this nightmare – to pass through the solid mass.

Brendon was still picking up the vibration, but then heard it become a roaring sound, like huge engines screaming, churning, burning as they ran out of control. It was deafening. His digital readings were off the scale. Steve must have heard it too. His hand was shaking but he kept on filming Becky as she tilted sideways, as if her body was being thrown sharply to one side. Steve was struggling to keep the camera on her.

Becky held on to a strap on the fuselage wall. 'It's going down!' she screamed.

The whole film crew could now hear screams that were not coming from Becky but saw nothing. Olly's monitor showed Becky bending to one side, hand clinging to a strap, her face twisted in terror.

'Steve, is everything okay?' asked Olly. Out there in the exhibition space, there wasn't a sound. Cantrell was standing by the open door of the aircraft, still on the walkway, but refusing to look inside. He had his hands over his ears.

Becky looked down the inside of the fuselage of the Lancaster. Through thick smoke, she saw the dead pilot slumped in the cockpit. His head was misshapen, and Becky realised that part of his skull was missing, blown away by enemy fire; the place where his ear and scalp should have been was mashed into tissue and bone, his brains splattered on the instrument panel in front of him. She smelled burning flesh and the coppery scent of human blood. A rush, almost a gale, of cold air blew through the fuselage. The Lancaster groaned and cracked, a splintering sound as the metal began to break up and the engines screamed out of control. Becky saw the still-surviving crewmen gripping the straps and screaming; one of them, only a boy, stared at her, his mouth quivering as his grip on the strap slipped and he was thrown like a rag doll towards the cockpit. Becky distinctly heard his neck break as he hit the floor.

Another airman, the flight engineer, his upper body covered in blood but his blue eyes still bright and alive in his blackened face, stared at Becky as he tried to crawl away from the cockpit. It was a useless exercise – he was being dragged backwards by the force of gravity and speed, what was left of one arm clawing at the aircraft floor. The smell of burning, scorched flesh intensified. The navigator was crying quietly as he clung to the chair at his post. Paper was flying around him, a photograph of a blonde woman, smiling and holding an infant, blown away in the rush of air. He was on fire, his uniform blazing, his sobs becoming loud screams as his flesh melted; he staggered out of the chair, lost his balance, and rolled away towards the cockpit, a blazing shape engulfed in flames, bumping on the floor and howling. It was unspeakable.

The final horror. Becky experienced the last moments of the aircraft, saw the ground getting nearer and nearer through the cockpit, and knew the Lancaster was about to be smashed into the earth. She braced herself; her body went rigid, her eyes closed, and her knees buckled.

Steve tried to keep filming. His camera was unsteady, and he was completely disorientated. Brendon was watching his digital sound feed, an expression of disbelief on his face.

And then it stopped.

There was silence, apart from Steve's ragged breathing. He could hear Olly in his ear.

'You okay? Great footage!'

Steve shifted the camera off his shoulder and headed for the door. 'Fuck this,' he said, as Brendon shuffled back onto the walkway on hands and knees, blubbering.

'What was that? Christ, what was that?'

Becky stood slumped against the fuselage. As she turned to get out of the infernal machine, she distinctly heard a voice whispering in her ear.

'We are here.'

Olly could not understand why the crew were gibbering wrecks. He had watched the footage on the monitor and Becky was fantastic. He watched Steve, shaking, emerge from the fuselage. He told Olly his hands were icy cold.

Olly was watching Cantrell trying to warm Becky's hands, rubbing them rather over-enthusiastically as he muttered, 'Sorry, so sorry.' Brendon seemed to be in shock, sitting as far away from the bomber as he could get, staring into space. He hadn't spoken since he ran down the metal walkway, his sound equipment still in his hands. Olly watched Becky; she was sitting in the chair she had used to interview Cantrell earlier. She was pale, her red hair shimmering in the arc lights while the Lancaster sat above her like a giant moth, waiting to swoop down on her. Olly had no idea what the matter with any of them was. His excitement to see what they had got on film was paramount.

He asked Steve to review the footage before Becky did a summary to the camera.

'All right, but I won't be going back in there, mate, whatever you say.' Steve was adamant. As they looked at the footage, Olly was astonished that at the point when Becky first said she felt a vibration and spoke of hearing the voices of men, her breath white in the cold air, the film became a jumpy series of faint images with what looked like massive interference, making the footage grainy and indistinct. Olly could not believe it. He had just watched the live feed, clear and distinct, in its entirety on the monitor. On playback, there were over four minutes of distorted images.

Steve was upset. 'I know what I saw, and I know I was recording.' Olly remembered the remote feed cameras – maybe they got something.

He spoke to Brendon. 'Tell me you have it,' he said, agitated. Brendon had worked for years in regional TV, where the worst things he ever had to record sound for were local floods and soap stars opening supermarkets. He was shaking.

'What?' he asked.

'Tell me you have that on sound – whatever went on in there.'

Brendon looked down at the equipment in his hand, his headphones slumped around his neck.

'Check it, for God's sake!' Olly sat on his haunches, looking Brendon in the eye. 'Come on, mate, Becky was acting it all up. Just check what you have.' Brendon, looking very pale, put his headphones back on and rewound the feed. As he listened, his face contorted with fear. He handed Olly a second set of headphones and both men sat and listened with incredulity. The sound recording was distinct: the steady hum of a vibration, then the screaming of the engine and Becky's voice, the rush of air coursing through the Lancaster and the screams, by God, the screams. Then nothing. Just silence before the sound of Becky and Steve getting out of the Lancaster. Brendon nodded, taking his headphones off and looking at Olly.

'Jesus Christ,' he said weakly.

'Well, thank God,' said Olly. 'At least we've got something.'

He told Steve to check the remote feed from the cameras inside the aircraft and walked over to where Becky and Cantrell were sitting beneath the wing of the Lancaster.

'We need to go back in. There was a problem with the film and—'

'No!' Becky and Cantrell spoke in unison.

Becky removed her hand from Cantrell's. She looked at Olly, tears in her eyes.

'You heard that, didn't you? And you must have seen it. I saw those men die, Olly, and I cannot, I will not watch that abomination again.'

Steve walked over to them. 'Same thing happened on the remote camera feeds,' he said to Olly, sounding puzzled. 'We have multiple shots of the inside until the same time as my camera goes down. Sorry, mate, it must be some kind of electrical interference. But I can tell you now, I'm not going back in there either.'

Olly looked at the assembled group and then back up at the Lancaster, silent and magnificent in the hangar. He calculated what they had recorded and knew he could edit it to create the sequence as if something supernatural had interrupted their filming. He also had the sound footage to go with it. He couldn't work out why the visual feeds were corrupted when Brandon had safely recorded the sound of whatever went on in there. He wondered whether Cantrell had deliberately sabotaged the filming somehow. But that didn't make any sense, either – there was nothing in it for him. He decided he could use the electrical interference to their advantage, suggesting that something unknown indeed happened here. Heck, it would go viral online and make the pilot for *The Cambridge Medium* the most talked about footage on all the wackjob Internet sites.

What Olly couldn't explain was the way Becky and the crew were reacting. He asked himself if he would step inside that bomber right now. He was ashamed to realise that, on balance, he would rather not.

'Okay,' Olly said slowly, 'Becky, we'll wrap this with you to the camera in here, explaining what you think happened inside. Steve, set the shot up here under the Lancaster's nose. Brendon, make sure she's wired for sound. Let's go in ten.'

Becky recorded the final piece to camera, standing beneath the bulbous front gun position, the Lancaster looming over her. She was pale, but Olly liked the fact that she looked slightly traumatised. It would add to the drama. She talked through what she experienced, and her narrative was emotional. She signed off, saying that this was a haunting the Cambridge Medium would never revisit.

It was not until Olly reviewed all the footage in the days after the trip to Lincolnshire that he was sure he could see a black shape, almost a shadow, standing in the cockpit of the Lancaster behind Becky.

He was looking at the final take and he spotted what may well have been a trick of the light. But when he enhanced the image and stopped the frame – the shadow was only on the footage for a couple of seconds – it looked as if the indistinct, black shape had a mouth, glowing red, with what appeared to be sharp white teeth. It disappeared almost as rapidly as it appeared. Olly remembered Becky's fear. He mentally shook himself and reminded himself that this was all just entertainment. The fact that he was working with one of the best was making him see things. Plus, there was some kind of electrical problem that must have caused the original footage to corrupt. That would explain the black smudge on the film.

He went back to editing the TV pilot, which was looking very convincing indeed.

CHAPTER THIRTEEN

Becky Moran was standing on the stage of the Dominion Theatre. The light surrounded her body, the spotlight beamed down on her. From behind, she was outlined in light but the shape and silhouette of her body were dark. There was a halo around the red hair, the light from above shafting out around her into the auditorium.

Becky saw the open cavern of the theatre space in front of her: rows and rows of empty seats, the two banked galleries ascending upwards, the darker pit below in the stalls, and the house lights dotted along the walls. Looking out from the stage, it appeared as though she was the only person in the theatre, framed by the light, projecting her essence outwards into her performance space, a womb-like cocoon into which Becky Moran would perform to two thousand people in a few hours' time.

'Great, Becky, thanks,' the lighting director told her. The sound had been checked. The stage was set with a simple series of twisted swathes of white cloth to create the backdrop, with lights fixed on the gantry above and directed onto the stage below, lights that would change colour throughout the show. They'd project shafts up and down the backdrop: pink, warm, and soft to begin with, then taking on a blue tinge when Becky did her psychic readings. Her name was also written in an elegant script on the backdrop. The effect when the curtain went up would be of light, space, and modernity. Hugh had designed it and it had served Becky well for major stage shows such as this.

Hugh was in his element. His love of live theatre and just being here in the Dominion made him feel completely at home. He was out front in the stalls, watching the lighting check and, for once, completely sober. He never drank on a show day. Well, that wasn't exactly true. He was usually to be seen necking vodka from his hipflask as the final curtain call ended when, by then, all had gone well. Within an hour of curtain down, he would not usually remember much at all of what had happened. This was a major venue, booked way in advance, as the theatre did not have many 'down days' between one long production ending and a new one beginning. Divine Diva had the Dominion for one day only.

Hugh had sent the mouldy one to make sure that front of house had the programmes.

Sarah's job this Sunday was to look after Becky and do whatever Hugh needed. She had arrived at the West End theatre on Tottenham Court Road in a cab and had lugged the programmes inside in cardboard boxes. The smell of mothballs surrounding Sarah was strong today. She was dressed in a vibrant red, white, and blue top with pink jeans, but she had a vintage outfit ready for tonight's show. Vintage meant Dorothy Perkins circa 2000, a multi-coloured striped jumpsuit worn with a pair of second-hand Doc Martins into which were threaded silver laces. The look was of a deranged plumber in a rather flamboyant mood, but Sarah loved it, imagining that she'd look like a black Kate Bush. If Hugh had heard that, he would have guffawed with some quip about a bush that needed trimming. Not to mention dry cleaning.

In Becky's dressing room, housed at the rear of the theatre, the signature black dress was on a padded hanger with the Louboutin heels placed on the floor below. Her make-up was laid out on a linen cloth, the make-up bag open with its expensive cosmetics arranged inside. Pre-prepared notes for some invited members of the audience were nearby inside a leather folder so that Becky could review what the research team had provided for some of the readings tonight. Hugh had insisted that the usual procedures should be in place, just in case this new-found gift of being a mouthpiece for the spirit world should abandon her the minute she stepped on stage in front of a full house of punters who had paid good money to see Becky Moran and hear from dead loved ones.

'We're taking no chances, Becky,' he'd told her. 'Let's give the people what they want.' Sarah was sure Becky wouldn't need the notes or the earpiece through which Hugh would feed her information about those in the audience who were desperate to have a message during the live show.

Hugh had invited Aiden O'Conner as a guest. O'Conner had insisted, grandly, that he wanted a seat in a box, so Sarah had been instructed to leave a glass of champagne and some chocolates for him there, the implication being that they were a gift from Becky.

'Shall I spit in the fizz, Becky?' Sarah had asked, quite seriously.

'Tempting, but no.' Becky had laughed. Sarah was a bit crestfallen. 'Leave him a bottle on ice instead,' Becky suggested.

'It's no good, I can't spit in that,' Sarah had said, morosely.

Sarah also reminded Becky that a journalist, Lulu LaBelle, was due to interview her that afternoon. Becky frowned. 'Hugh said it was as well to get it done today – the woman has seats tonight – she can write the piece up as "An Encounter with the Cambridge Medium".' Sarah rolled her eyes. 'I think she may be as mad as a snake – she has been so excited about meeting you all week. Do you want me to come with you?' Becky shook her head.

'I can manage, Sarah. Where am I meeting her?'

Sarah looked at her notes. 'Coffee at Starbucks down Tottenham Court Road then back here for the interview. I'll make sure she's out of here after half an hour, so you can dress and relax before the show. What time are your parents arriving?'

Becky said they would come to the stage door of the Dominion after four, after they'd had lunch at The Ritz. 'I'll make sure Security know and meet them there.'

Sarah made sure all Becky's notes for tonight were in order and fussed over her. 'Are you sure I can't spit in O'Conner's fizz?' she asked. The women both burst out laughing.

Olly wasn't working that day at the Dominion because the stage shows were Hugh's speciality. A film crew would do some stage shots to use in the TV pilot, but they were straightforward, allowing Olly to spend the weekend editing the material they had filmed in Lincolnshire.

He had talked through the technical problems with the TV footage from inside the Lancaster with Hugh and shared his plan to spook up the edit, so it looked as though a supernatural force had interfered with the filming. Hugh had agreed, as puzzled as Olly about why some of the visual footage was ruined yet the sound recording remained intact, with some very strange noises and sound effects that Olly could not explain. He'd also told Hugh that the film crew wouldn't go back in the Lancaster to de-rig the equipment in the dark. Hugh muttered darkly that they wouldn't get paid for a second day's shift, so Olly said he would leave that for Hugh to sort out.

Olly had driven Becky to London from the airfield late that Thursday night. They were both very tired, but Becky had been particularly quiet. Olly wanted to run through Friday's *Medium Wave* line-up as they drove, but she didn't want to talk. As they passed Watford on the M1, Olly had finally asked her what had gone on in that Lancaster bomber.

'Death,' said Becky, bleakly. 'And I saw it, all of it.'

Olly had sighed, not quite sure he would ever understand this woman, who communicated to thousands with her at first faked and now, apparently, real ability to see the Other Side.

'You need to have some fun, Becky, you work too hard. Get a boyfriend, get laid, get drunk.' Becky looked at Olly. Her eyes were sad and then she had turned her head away and looked out on the motorway, the lights whizzing past the old Land Rover.

The team had assembled at the Cube the next day for their weekly radio show. The guest list that evening included another so-called psychic fortune teller called Rita Orlando, from Bath. Some called her 'Robbing Rita' as she had a documented habit of taking a client's money and throwing them out if they questioned her. She had a Naughty Step in her house, too, where a client could end up if they wound her up. Apparently, the step was almost always occupied, and yet she'd had some successes, with a track record in prophecy. The rumour was that she had predicted three Grand National winners and the exact dates of birth and names of the last two royal babies. Her clients came clutching lottery tickets. They usually ended up on the Naughty Step within thirty seconds.

A cellist with the London Philharmonic was also coming in. He had authored several respected books on UFO activity worldwide and had even spoken on Capitol Hill, Washington, about the UFO phenomenon and conspiracy theories. He claimed to have met an alien back in the nineties, an alien dressed in a trilby hat, while he was rehearsing a concert at Carnegie Hall. The musician said he'd known it was an ET because the other-worldly humanoid had touched his nose in a knowing way. Some sort of pre-arranged signal. Hugh said the New York alien sounded more like a wartime spiv selling nylons.

Finally, there was an Irishwoman whose books were international bestsellers and who said she could see angels. Lots of them. All the time. Her gift was an ability to communicate with these angelic hosts whilst her Catholic faith simultaneously brought reassurance to millions. Her gentle southern Irish accent reassured everyone that they had a Guardian Angel, always looking after them. The angel business was huge, and Olly knew her appearance would be a ratings magnet.

Tonight, the radio show had passed off without incident. The team had parted after a drink at the Soho Club, knowing that the stage show at the Dominion on Sunday was going to be a great success. Hugh was delighted that the show was sold out. He'd left the club that Friday night, full of vodka, a handsome, muscular young man on one arm. He was smiling and waving at his team as he and his date headed off to his London flat.

Lulu LaBelle (real name Louise Longbottom, but you can't work in show business with a name like that) had already arrived at Starbucks, ready to meet Britain's most famous psychic medium, Becky Moran.

Her business card read, in italics: ***Lulu LaBelle – Showbiz Journalist.*** There was a small ink drawing of an old-fashioned upright typewriter, in case you missed the point. Embossed on a lilac background, Lulu would produce this card in a cloud of Chanel No. 5 at any opportunity. The card usually came with a gushing narrative, such as, 'Showbiz journo. Lunches, launches, gala dinners, and awards ceremonies!' Gushing worked for Lulu. She had mastered the art. She was a top celebrity journalist, her byline and uncritical articles on soap stars, pop stars and the wealthy appeared in all the top-selling magazines and popular press. She was known on the circuit by anxious managers and stars to be a safe pair of hands, flattering and sympathetic. Lulu had learned that was how to get the interviews that would sell.

A round woman, Lulu had never found being what the magazines called 'plus size' a problem. 'Drape,' they said, and Lulu draped herself in as much multi-coloured cloth as she could wrap around her. She was now almost forty, she wore her hair long, crinkly, a shade of faded blonde. Her glasses were also red, framed with horn-rimmed diamanté. Very short-sighted, she used a magnifying mirror to apply her make-up. As a result, the eyeshadow was a bit patchy today, the eyeliner wonky, and the lipstick (Dior Red) slightly missed her mouth. It didn't look too good smeared on her teeth, either.

As Lulu waited, she glanced at her knock-off Prada handbag (last season). In there was her digital recorder, reporter notepad, and a pen. She was early. She was due to meet Becky at half past two, but she wanted to be ready. This piece was for the glossy weekly *Stars and Their Lives*, but Lulu thought she could also knock off a profile piece for the *Daily Mail*. It had been hard to find much to research about Becky Moran. She rarely gave any interviews. Not that actual research bothered Lulu. She knew her interviewing skills would draw out this mysterious woman who apparently could talk to the dead.

Lulu had listened to Becky's radio show on Friday night. She was looking forward to seeing the live stage show tonight. She just knew she and Becky would be very good friends. Looking on her website, there was a superb black and white photograph of Becky Moran in her unique, classic style: wearing a slightly off-the-shoulder, slim-fitting black dress with her hair swooped down over her shoulders. She wore no jewellery. The smile was enigmatic. Lulu thought Becky looked as if she should be on the cover of Vogue. She knew she had been to Cambridge, that her reputation as a psychic was astonishing, and – the reason she had got this interview – it was rumoured that she was about to make a TV show called *The Cambridge Medium*.

Becky Moran's stage shows were sell-outs, with audiences full of wonder about what Becky heard from the Other Side. Lulu had VIP tickets to the Dominion and she was sure that Becky would throw in a free reading for her this afternoon as part of the interview. They were going to be such good friends.

Lulu smiled. She had bought a new outfit. The saleswoman in Bon Marché had described the garment's colour as aubergine, and Lulu had draped herself in yards of the shiny, deep purple, clinging Lycra, not noticing that it made her straggly blonde hair look slightly green and her skin sallow. She looked at herself in the shop's dressing room mirror and only saw a vision of undulating, curvy beauty. The fact that she may look to others like an overripe, rotting vegetable never even occurred to her. As she dressed that Sunday morning, Lulu had prised the copy pair of white Louboutin stilettos with the red soles on to her feet, ignoring the pain and the sheer difficulty of walking. Instead of a coat, Lulu draped a white faux fur wrap over her shoulders and just knew she looked amazing. From the rear, Lulu's backside resembled two pigs fighting in a shiny, purple sack.

She was slightly annoyed that the *Mail* had got the exclusive with Becky a week ago, after that unicorn man had attacked her live on air at The Voice of Britain. Lulu had emailed Hugh to tell him she could have done a better job with that interview for him and that he should always think of her first. Hugh had not even replied, which Lulu thought very ill-mannered. After all, her article in *Stars and Their Lives* would be massive. She would speak to Becky about it. She slid her red diamanté horn-rimmed spectacles onto her nose, applied her trademark red lipstick, and pouted at the mirror.

Becky was sitting in her dressing room, drinking some water before heading out to meet LaBelle. She was thinking that she should not have arranged to do this on the day of a show, but it had seemed a good idea at the time. Since Olly had dropped her off at the hotel in Covent Garden very late on Thursday night, Becky had been feeling exhausted. Those few minutes witnessing the horror on the Lancaster bomber had drained her beyond measure. And the sharp fear she'd felt, hearing that whispered voice saying, 'We are here' as she stumbled out of the fuselage, had almost sent her over the edge. She had slept with all the lights on again, imagining a white aura all around her body, and wearing her amulet to ward off whatever was haunting her. Sleep had not come easily. Every time she closed her eyes, she'd seen those airmen in their final few agonising seconds of life. Becky still felt physically sick, still smelled the burning flesh.

Whatever this thing that she had was, it was not a gift at all. It was a curse. Now, she had to summon the energy to perform on stage in this theatre. Becky used to love the stage shows, the response of a big audience, the applause. Now, she felt old and weary. She had woken that Sunday morning feeling on edge, feeling there was something she should remember, just out of her grasp. This feeling worried her – her intuition was highly developed now – but she put it down to being tired and overwhelmed by the events of the last three weeks.

She suddenly remembered too that her parents would be here, and she groaned at the thought of her mother in her powder-blue trouser suit, telling everyone that Becky was her daughter. Her dad would just look uncomfortable and disapproving. Becky sighed, stood up, and pulled on her black coat. Picking up her small handbag, she headed out into Tottenham Court Road.

'Becky! Becky! Here I am!' LaBelle was waving a purple arm in Becky's direction, the white fake fur slipping off her shoulder and dangling onto the dirty London pavement. Lulu tottered towards Becky, her feet splaying out over the sides of her cheap shoes, her ankles turning as the heels bent inwards, challenged by the weight they were carrying. She launched herself at Becky, planting a wonky lipstick mouth firmly on one cheek, then another, the scent of Chanel No. 5, sweet and heavy, wafting out from her rolling frame. Becky tried to step back, appalled at such a gush, such a display. It was useless. Lulu was like a ball of deconstructed energy, relentlessly bearing down.

Becky tried to smile and failed, but Lulu didn't seem to notice.

'Here we are! Girls together. And you are going to tell my fortune! It had better be good. Let's get a coffee and a catch-up!'

Becky tried to wipe the red smears of lipstick from both sides of her face, whilst at the same time trying to get Lulu's hand off her wrist as she pulled Becky into Starbucks. Inside, for once, there was no queue at the counter. LaBelle let go of Becky's arm and was already staring at the cake selection.

'I shall have a skinny latte and one of those.' Lulu pointed at a huge wedge of carrot cake. 'What about you, Bex?' She beamed at Becky, lipstick-smeared teeth visible above the purple Lycra.

'My name is Becky, Lulu, and I'll have a double espresso, please.' She went to sit down at a nearby table. Lulu followed her after waiting to watch the barista concoct the steam, milk, and coffee with a flourish.

'I know I shouldn't, but the cake is so good in here,' Lulu gushed as she sat down. 'Don't you eat before a show? I suppose it's in case you throw up?' Lulu emptied four sachets of sugar into her skinny latte and started to dig at the cake with a fork, stuffing it in her mouth so that the cream-cheese icing smeared another layer over the lipstick. Her other hand pushed her red sparkly glasses up towards the bridge of her nose. 'I read that every great actor gets stage fright. Christopher Biggins once threw up in his wig just before he went on stage as Widow Twanky in panto. He still went on, though. In the wig. That's showbiz! Do you get like that, Bex?'

'Lulu, please don't call me Bex. My name is Becky.' She sipped her espresso. 'No, I don't get stage fright. And, by the way, I don't tell fortunes, I speak with spirits. It's lovely to meet you – how are you, Lulu?'

Lulu set off on a breathless rant about lunches, launches, and showbiz dinners. She was in full flow, eating with her mouth open, her animated face chewing and talking and spitting bits of carrot cake in different directions. Becky noticed an attractive man sitting at the next table, watching the tableau with great amusement. He smiled at Becky and made a sympathetic face. Becky nodded. He stood up.

'Ladies,' the accent was French, 'excuse me, but are you the famous Becky Moran?' Lulu stopped chewing, obviously surprised at this vision of sophisticated loveliness standing by the table. Her mouth remained open, cream cheese on her chin. She looked at Becky, who was handling this as if it happened every Sunday afternoon at a quarter to three in Starbucks on Tottenham Court Road. Lulu thought he looked like George Clooney playing a French diplomat, the version of George Clooney that didn't involve a beard but did involve a tuxedo, dark hair, and a chiselled jaw. Her mouth was still open. The

Frenchman produced a card and handed it to Becky, ignoring Lulu apart from a short nod of acknowledgement. 'I am coming to your show this evening, Ms Moran,' he said. 'I am a great admirer. Would you ask your people to contact me, so I may have a reading?' His English was near perfect.

Becky looked at the card with the Mayfair address.

'Thank you, Monsieur Bertrand, it will be my pleasure.' Becky smiled as he took her hand.

'François, call me François, please.'

Lulu looked towards his left hand. 'You're married, then?' she asked.

Becky threw her a sharp look. 'I'll get my office to call you and I hope you enjoy the show this evening,' she said, her hand still in his.

'*Merci*, I am looking forward to it. Have a nice afternoon, ladies.' He let go of Becky's hand and swept out of the coffee shop.

'Cheek of it, Bex!' Lulu was indignant, her demeanour jealous and annoyed. 'He'll be after that *cinq-à-sept*. Bet he has six kids and a string of women up and down London.'

'*Cinq-à-sept*? What on Earth is that?'

Lulu gave Becky a knowing look. 'It's five-til-seven, the two hours in the day that the Frenchies see their mistresses. Well known, Bex.' Lulu nodded sagely, the white faux fur sliding off her shoulders again. Becky decided she had had enough. She stood up, putting the business card into her bag.

'Let's go and do the interview, Lulu.' Lulu forked the last piece of cake into her mouth and gulped down her latte, hooking up with Becky's arm as she stood. 'Isn't this great?' She beamed.

Becky had been watching a spirit, a small woman, standing with Lulu, wearing a pinafore and watching Lulu with complete exasperation. Becky knew it was Lulu's dead grandmother. Before François had come over, the woman was telling Becky that 'our Louise needs to knock it off'. She was apologising to Becky for the ridiculous way her granddaughter was carrying on. She had watched Louise stuff the cake down and told Becky she was just pretending to be someone she was not, called her a greedy girl, and said she always had been. The spirit was telling Becky that Louise hadn't been brought up this way. She would bat Lulu over the head every so often, though the spirit hand was unseen and unfelt by Lulu. Becky wondered how she was going to tell Lulu that dead Granny was watching, and dead Granny wasn't at all pleased.

What puzzled Becky was that the spirit now seemed to be getting agitated, glancing around. Becky frowned as the spirit spoke to her, but she could no longer understand what she was saying. Then she just faded away, her arms outstretched towards Lulu.

It didn't make any sense.

Becky opened the door, with Lulu clinging to her arm as if it were welded, and the two women walked down Tottenham Court Road towards the Dominion. Becky explained to Lulu that she would have to sign her in at the stage door and they would want to see some ID. Lulu nodded and said she had her NUJ card in her purse. Tottenham Court Road was busy, the traffic heavy, and the streets packed with Sunday afternoon shoppers and tourists.

CHAPTER FOURTEEN

The screams started just after the gunshots.

A man carrying a four-year-old girl watched as a slim, very smart looking redhead in a black coat, and a larger woman, wearing a purple dress and a white fur stole, was gunned down in front of him. The gunman, the witness told the police later, had just stepped out onto Tottenham Court Road holding a pistol. He was wearing a hoodie. The man had passed in front of him and his child on the street and walked calmly up to the two women, who looked as though they were heading to the stage door of the Dominion. The gunman had raised his pistol, shouted something – no, the witness couldn't make out what – and when the two women turned around to face him he'd aimed the pistol at the redhead and fired. The witness saw her blood spatter onto the white fur wrap and the woman wearing it had cried out in terror. The redhead fell to the pavement.

Then the gunman had calmly turned towards the woman in purple and fired, point blank, at her.

The witness hadn't seen the gunman's face because he was in shock, staring in disbelief and in utter fear at the women he had just watched being shot right in front of him and his daughter. He was holding his child, covering her body with his arms to protect her, sure in that second that the gunman would turn on him and his child too in a massacre similar to what had happened in Paris.

He had frozen, but his child had started to scream. The gunman, however, had lowered the weapon and just walked away, his head down and covered by the hoodie. He'd walked slowly down Tottenham Court Road. He must have been splattered with blood, the witness said.

He was shaking as he described other passers-by rushing over to the women who had been shot, whilst he heard voices shouting, 'Call the police, call an ambulance!'

The witness described someone was attempting CPR on the redhead but, clearly, the one in the purple dress was beyond saving. Her blood was pumping all over the white fur, he heard another bystander tell her companion. It was drenched. Later, the witness told the police officer, over and over, that it was like watching what happens when they club a baby seal to death. That was all he could think of.

People ran out of the Dominion Theatre. There was a black woman in brightly-coloured clothes, calling out a name, and a tall, white, thin chap in a suit. They must have heard the gunfire. They ran over to where the two women who had been shot were splayed out on the pavement, yelling for help. They got on their knees in all that blood, calling out the redhead's name, holding her. Someone else was trying to stem the blood, trying to save her. Just a passer-by.

A witness said that the two who'd run out of the theatre was completely smeared with blood. It was on their hands and clothes, in their hair, everywhere, as they knelt by the victims. By the time the ambulance arrived, the tall man was sobbing, holding the redhead's hand and saying her name. It was 'Becky', the witness was sure that was what he said.

'She's dead, Sarah,' he kept saying. 'Becky is dead.'

CHAPTER FIFTEEN

Becky Moran opens her eyes.

She sees a clear glass bubble suspended in front of her. There is a swirl of white mist trapped inside the globe. The mist meets the inner glass surface of the perfect sphere and lingers for a short while, then swirls back into the globe. The vapour is constantly moving, and Becky finds her whole attention is focused on this bubble. It is hanging in a clear, icy blue light and seems to be floating. Becky could stretch out her hand and touch the surface of the glass globe. It would be cool, smooth, and delicate. Becky could put her hand underneath the bauble and hold it. It would sit, cupped in her hand. The haze trapped inside the glass has a dynamic of its own. Swirling, cascading but gentle. The mist is white, it neither reflects nor absorbs that blue light surrounding it. Becky wants to discover what it is, understand it, rationalise it, examine it, this droplet, this globule of whirling, rolling glass, surrounded by a sheen of blue-tinged light.

No, there is more. Becky feels a sense of peace and tranquillity. She is unburdened, almost as if she is floating, weightless, like a feather. Gravity has gone, and she has slipped into some unseen bond with the Earth itself. There is warmth, gentle and enveloping. Serenity and joy combine to make Becky feel happy. There is just her and the glass bubble. No noise. No pain.

As Becky registers this absence of pain, a memory of a hot blast of searing agony in her body shakes the equilibrium. The glass globe begins to float away and the feeling of serene comfort, suspended in this clear blue atmosphere, diminishes. Yes, there was pain, such pain. Becky sees the light change and feels gravity connecting with her body again. Fear replaces the tranquillity and Becky is confused.

She can see the glass bubble ahead, far ahead now. The outer rim of the sphere is still shimmering as the light is fading, but it is no longer within her hand's reach. She raises her arm, reaching, yearning for it to come back so she can touch that round surface and watch the swirls within. As she reaches, her being moves back towards the globe. Becky's need to be with this object is strong. She can feel the opposing pull downwards, almost as if the ground does not want her to move, but to stay, stay here; yet she resists, stretching towards the bubble that is waiting for her.

There is no sound. Becky realises she is moving without the use of her limbs. She looks down and sees that her body is there. But she can propel herself without walking. All she has to do is reach, reach more, and she can move, she can float. Becky needs to get back to that sense of peace, to get to it, hold it, and embrace it. The force that is holding her back gives, just a little.

She looks ahead of her into the infinity, but the sphere is now very small, very distant. She wants to cry out that it should wait, it should stay and not leave her here. Then Becky feels an overwhelming sense of sadness and of loss, of abandonment.

The bubble vanishes.

The paramedics arrived quickly, running to where Becky and Lulu lay on the ground. The police were already setting up a cordon and moving the onlookers away from the carnage on Tottenham Court Road. Hugh got up, holding on to Sarah for support as the medics attended to Becky, seeing that Lulu was beyond their help. There was chaos. Hugh thought he had stepped into a nightmare beyond any comprehension; he held Sarah's arm very tightly.

Sarah was in shock, her face twisted, her hand shaking. Neither noticed the blood on their clothing, the smell of it, nor its visceral texture smearing their hands. They stared at Becky, the smart, beautiful redhead now no longer a person. Now she looked like a slaughtered marionette, lifeless and motionless on the pavement. A pool of almost black blood stained the ground she lay on, mingling with the blood from Lulu LaBelle.

One team moved in to put Lulu on a gurney while another team attached a drip to Becky and were quickly working to get her into another ambulance.

'What's her name?' the paramedic asked as he worked on Becky. Sarah answered, as Hugh stared at the teams who were moving fast to get the victims of this shooting to hospital. Hugh could not speak. Sarah told them about Lulu too. She asked if she could come in the ambulance. Hugh looked at her, startled, allowing her to take control.

'Hugh, listen to me. Call Olly, tell him what's happened, make him come and sort out what we need to do now.' Sarah moved with the paramedics, rushing to get Becky into the ambulance, fighting for her life. 'Hugh, do it now. I am going with Becky.' The paramedics told Sarah she couldn't come in the ambulance as they had some serious work to do, but she should come to A&E at University College Hospital and wait there. She ran to get a cab, shouting behind her, 'Hugh! Call Olly now.'

The ambulance pulled away at speed, with Becky inside. The one carrying Lulu followed, but no one was under any illusion that she could be saved.

Hugh looked at the stains on the pavement and then saw for the first time the blood covering his own body; he saw the armed police officers, the uniformed men and women already talking to witnesses, he heard the babble of the police radios coordinating the search for the gunman. He became aware of the scream of sirens, the sound of London all around him, the people gawping, the police tape, and the backdrop of the Dominion Theatre with the three-metre-high banner 'An Evening with the Cambridge Medium, Becky Moran' hanging above the main entrance.

Then he noticed a couple trying to get through the police cordon. The woman was dressed in a powder-blue trouser suit and was shouting. Hugh realised his brain was operating on two levels: one frozen in shock and unbelief at what he had just seen and the other running as normal in an automatic response to his environment. Hugh recognised Becky's parents.

They met his eyes. Iris began to scream.

This corridor, dark and gloomy, in which Becky is now standing, is long and narrow. She feels cold. It's a deep chill that numbs the toes and the fingers. It makes her gasp for breath. A coldness that takes the moisture from her eyelashes, turning them white. Glacial air, penetrating, piercing, cutting, relentless.

Bitter air. Silence.

Becky turns around, but there is no way back. A wall, hewn with ice, is behind her. She looks ahead. The way forward, the only place to go, is a long, dimly lit path. In the distance, so far,

far away, she can see a small circle of light. Her hands, numb with the lack of any warmth, rise to touch the walls, so near to her that she doesn't need to stretch out her arms. The walls undulate and shimmer as if Becky is touching an icy membrane. Ripples cascade out from where her hands meet the surface. With one finger, she presses again into this nebulous barrier. Bright light splays out from the point of contact, but the substance resists her pressure.

Becky wants to be warm. She begins to move. There is that sensation again of propulsion rather than actually walking and it is that which is taking her forward. She looks down at her bare feet, gliding on a dull surface. She looks up and ahead, wanting, hoping to see that glass sphere, needing to find that elusive bubble.

This corridor... no, that's not right, she thinks. Perhaps she is in a tunnel? Looking up, there is a low, arched roof that may be made of stone, and the narrow space ahead of her is very long. She knows she is moving, she feels herself moving, but that small circle of light ahead does not change in size.

She feels heavy, as if the gravity that her body has naturally negotiated during her life has suddenly become a burden, a force she has to resist, to fight, and to conquer. The very effort of movement is being made harder, she is being weighed down.

Becky looks behind her. In the gloom, the wall has been swallowed up. She has no idea of how far she has moved forward. Agitation begins to build up inside her. Yes, there was pain, she remembers it briefly and she tries to hurry forward as if to get away from that memory. She yearns for some warmth, some comfort.

Then, a sound. A slight vibration in the cold air.

She stands still. No, it's more of a rumble, deeper; she feels it, the sound is being absorbed by the dull floor. Becky is disorientated, she can't hear where the sound is coming from, this vibration, this roll of sound, this oscillation, this deep soundwave. Then it begins to take on a rhythm. Low, solid, repetitive, Becky feels the narrow space she occupies is becoming a conduit, an instrument in itself, perhaps even the creator of this percussive noise. She stands, her bones and cartilage, her muscles and soft tissue, her very flesh absorbing the shockwaves of sound that are now louder. She becomes afraid, recognising the sound. She is becoming that sound: a deep thrum, thrum, thrum, and she is being absorbed by it.

The trauma team in the ambulance struggled to keep Becky stable, to stem the huge blood loss and make sure her heart kept beating. The paramedic shouted at the driver to go faster. An emergency team was waiting for them at University College Hospital and they needed to get there quickly. The siren wailed over Warren Street. It was twenty past three in the afternoon.

Iris and Peter were being escorted to the hospital by a police liaison officer. Hugh had faced Becky's parents with her blood smeared on his hands and clothes and smudged on his face. He felt very old. He told them all he knew, that he'd heard gunshots and had run outside. Peter had shouted at Hugh, blaming him, saying that he knew all this rubbish wasn't what his girl should be doing. Iris had begged to get to the hospital, begged to see her daughter, trying not to look at the blood, still fresh and staining the pavement in front of her. The police had come and taken Iris and Peter away. Hugh was in shock and didn't seem able to move. The police had wrapped him in a foil blanket and led him away to talk to them about what he saw, what he knew, because the gunman was still out there.

Olly picked up the text from Sarah as he stood up in the Soho TV edit suite that Divine Diva had hired from an independent production house in Wedgewood Mews, on Greek Street. At that very moment, Olly was looking at the frame of footage of the black shape with a red mouth, in the cockpit of the Lancaster, and asking the technician what he made of it. Olly read the short message, grabbed his jacket, and ran out of the door. There were tears of shock in his eyes.

As the ambulance turned into Euston Road, the alarm system monitoring Becky's vital signs beeped out a warning.
'We're losing her!'
The team moved quickly and calmly to try and restart Becky's heart.

'We are here.'

Becky hears them.

The cacophony of noise is now all around her. She is absorbing that rotting smell, sweetly decaying, the stench of rotting flesh, fly-blown and ancient. It is the smell of the charnel house, the plague pit, the foul odour of the ditch where the executed are thrown, then to be doused in quicklime, their broken bodies foaming as they are covered by the very soil they removed as they dug their own graves.

The tunnel is expanding now. But there is no circle of light ahead. Becky is now suspended where the very contours of space are undulating. It is a place of shadows with no visible light, just a pall of dim, red dullness accentuating the shifting shapes all around her. It is as if the matrix of reality is being corrupted.

'We are here, we are here, and we are here.' The voices have become a demonic chant, a choir of primordial voices, the many blending as one. The voices chant as the deep thrum, thrum, thrum becomes louder. Becky watches the floor shape-shifting beneath her, aware that her physical body is weightless. The red tinge deepens, expands, and contracts in time with the thrum, thrum, thrum.

The stench makes the air sticky and thick. There had been such a sense of peace and of lightness before when that glass sphere was in front of her. Now her being, her humanity, is being eradicated. She feels the fabric of this desolation wrapping itself around her, seeping through her skin and crawling under her fingernails, caressing her feet almost like the touch of a lover, steady, silky, beguiling.

The choir chants its evil anthem louder, relentlessly. Her senses are locked into the thrum, thrum, thrum, accompanied by that hypnotic throb of the dull redness, with the shadows growing darker. She thinks she can see shapes in the shadows. It is as if they are waiting, moving nearer when the red pall recedes and holding back when it returns.

Becky knows they are here for her. They have always been here. Waiting.

Now, she is being enveloped by something with a hunger, a deep hunger. She watches a shadow begin to push through the shifting floor, stretching the surface under her feet as if it is a rotting membrane. The mucous surface, organic, a thin embryonic sac, is being pushed, stretched, elasticised by a force that is determined to rip it, push it aside, split it open.

Black strands of shadow break through, rising slowly. It is unlike the sly shapes around her in this space, which are hiding and indistinct, almost as if they are being kept under control. Becky sees this shadow rise like a dictator, a king, a commander, from below. It builds upwards, indistinct at first, an obscuration of form hewn out of darkness. The choir's voices become faster, frantic. Becky watches, fear blocking any thought process. Her soul is to be drawn from her. This shape-shifting, amorphous dark mass will absorb her.

'We are here,' chants the choir, faster and faster. Strands of darkness fly out from the shape that is gathering form in front of her. Shards of the ripped membrane – curling, dead, shrivelled – fall to the floor.

This thing has no defined shape. Whatever energy exists within it, it cannot settle on a shape. The strands of darkness curl out and then wrap back inwards. The bulk of the shadow becomes concave, then bulbous, the height building in on itself but lacking any skeletal structure to wrap itself around. There are no eyes, no clearly defined head shape. It is creating itself from darkness, like a swirl of ebony ink dropped into a vat of putrid water, spreading silently.

Then Becky sees, as the dark form undulates in front of her, that open red maw of a mouth, the teeth, sharp and white and dripping, dear God, dripping and glistening in the gloom.

The doors of the ambulance banged open as the Casualty team at University College Hospital rushed to take Becky inside. The paramedic, who had been in constant contact with the hospital in the few dramatic minutes of their journey, called out Becky's name and recited the failing vital statistics of his patient, telling them that her heart had stopped once, as the nurses and a doctor took the gurney, one holding the drip up high, the tube attached to Becky's arm, and raced at high speed down to theatre where surgeons were waiting, scrubbed up and ready to try to save the life of Becky Moran.

The second ambulance arrived. There was no rush here. Lulu LaBelle had been pronounced dead at the scene of the shooting. Her body was brought inside, to be taken to the mortuary for formal identification, covered by a bloodstained sheet.

Sarah rushed into A&E a few minutes after Becky had gone into theatre. There was a queue, the department busy. Sarah rushed ahead, excusing herself to those in line. The reception nurse took one look at her, smeared with blood, assumed she was injured, and let her push in. Sarah was crying, desperate to be with Becky and to find out where she was and if she was still alive. Once it had been established that Sarah was not hurt herself and that she was an associate of a victim, the nurse became indifferent.

'Spell the name, please,' she said, then asked what relationship Sarah was to Becky. The question hurt Sarah, who felt that Becky was her family; she was her friend. But that wouldn't do here, and Sarah was told that only family members would be informed what was happening, when there was any news. Sarah could always wait. She was told to take a seat and was shown where the ladies' bathroom was situated so she could clean herself up. The reception nurse was cool. Sarah wanted to reach through that glass screen and throttle her.

The receptionist knew from experience that the police would be here shortly and, no doubt, the real family members. Then the system would take over. She had no idea who this Becky Moran was. In a city used to murder, shootings, stabbings, and explosions, this was just another victim of crime. Another day of tragedy. Detached, she returned to processing the endless stream of patients coming into this overworked A&E and longs for the end of her shift.

'Next?' she called.

Iris and Peter were taken by the police to the hospital and to a waiting area by the theatre. Pale-green double doors faced them as they turned right into a small room. Their only child was behind those double doors, fighting for her life. Peter was grim-faced, Iris white. At the sight of the clinical room, anonymous, a wilting pot plant in the corner, and hard, plastic chairs, Iris became hysterical. Peter couldn't calm her nor stop her from crying out Becky's name. The female police officer, Dawn, went to find someone to sedate Iris while her colleague tried to find out if there was any news about their daughter. Dawn was aware that there was a manhunt going on in central London for the gunman; her focus, however, was on the family of this victim. She had been told that the other woman who was shot was dead and that the investigating team were trying to contact her next of kin. She did not tell the Moran parents about this. She found a nurse, who tried to calm Iris down.

There was no news from the operating theatre. Everyone waited.

Becky can feel pain. Her eyes are fixed on the entity hovering in front her, but she feels physical pain, a signal from the body she thought was no longer connected to her. The pain is sharp and overwhelming and, as it gets stronger, the dark shape diminishes a little. The wound of a mouth that wants to feed on her is drawing back, the drool sliding, dripping back into the crimson, and she can sense great anger as the voices of the many chants in outrage, querulous, denied.

'We are here! We are here!'

Becky feels herself being forced backwards at speed, away from the nebulous space, almost as if being rewound, and now she sees brightness sliding above her head as if she is looking upwards at strips of light on a ceiling. She is moving backwards, aware that she is on her back. Someone is saying her name. They seem to be shouting at her, willing her to respond. She smells antiseptic, she smells her own world, and she sees a shimmering light. The pain is now slamming into her body. Then any energy she had, even to blink, leaves her. She knows she has to fight, to stop any return to that dark place. She remembers the light that once saved her.

Then her world just ceases to be.

Olly arrived at the Dominion and was allowed past the police cordon as a member of the Divine Diva team just after he'd barged through the hordes of press. TV reporters were lined up on Tottenham Court Road, a TV crew were already broadcasting live, and London was on the hunt for the gunman. A reporter from The Voice of Britain was shouting after Olly.

'Olly! Mate! Give me a break!' The reporter was demanding access inside and an interview. Olly felt hunted, even though he himself was part of the media circus. He ignored the scrum.

The theatre manager, Eric, told Olly where to find Hugh. His team were busy cancelling tonight's show and needed help with drafting a statement to ticket holders and the press. Olly told Eric he'd get back to him in a moment and shouted at the crew to de-rig. They were all in a state of shock. They wanted news of Becky and the other woman. Olly knew nothing, despite texting Sarah on his way over to the Dominion. Sarah was at the hospital, Becky was in the operating theatre, and that was all he knew.

Olly found Hugh slumped in a chair in Becky's dressing room, a bottle of vodka in his hand. The police had taken his statement and let him return inside. Hugh knew the shooter was Brookings, he recognised what the witnesses had told the police and, of course, there had been his attempted attack on Becky at the Cube not nine days ago. Brookings was off the scale as far as Hugh was concerned, but he never imagined he was capable of murder. Brookings would have shot him too if he had been with Becky.

No one could know whether Brookings was coming back.

Hugh glugged his pale, clear, liquid friend. Becky... all they had done, the years of it, and now she'd been gunned down. Hugh felt guilt and fear and sorrow all at once. He raised the bottle as Olly walked in.

'The spirits couldn't save her,' he said, slurring. 'Not even this one.' He took another swig from the bottle. Olly walked over to him and gently took the bottle out of Hugh's hand. He put it on the dressing room table, next to Becky's make-up, laid out on the linen cloth. Hugh gazed sideways at the bottle sadly. Olly bent down towards him, speaking softly and slowly, using his hand to turn Hugh's face towards his own.

'Hugh, Becky may be dead. I have no idea about the other woman. But our friend is in surgery and may not survive while whoever did this is still out there. If you care for Becky, if you care for any of us, you get on your fucking feet, see to the mess in this theatre, honour all that Becky has done and get a fucking grip.'

Olly stood up. 'I'm telling you now, if you don't, I will drag you outside and I will beat the living shit out of you in front of the press. Don't think I won't. I have nothing to lose. Get a grip and do it now. And as for this stuff' –Olly threw the bottle of vodka against the dressing room wall– 'I may work for an alcoholic, but I'll be damned if I will work for an alcoholic with no balls. Becky deserves so much better than you.'

Hugh watched the vodka drip down the wall, the glass from the broken bottle lying smashed in a glittering, scattered pile. He hung his head and sobbed.

CHAPTER SIXTEEN

The strip lights are bright, synthetic, and harsh as they illuminate every corner of the operating theatre. Becky Moran is looking down at herself.

She sees herself lying on a table in the operating theatre. Her body is hooked up to machines and drips. A team of medics in scrubs are working over her, obscuring her view, and she wants them to move to one side, so she can see better. From up above, she moves her head to try and get a good view.

There is a team of six. An anaesthetist monitors her breathing, sitting in front of an illuminated screen near her head. She can see his forehead creased with lines of concentration and hear a machine rasp mechanically as it pushes oxygen into her, mimicking her breath. Becky sees her own hair is wrapped away in what looks like a shower cap and there is a tube sticking out of her mouth. She can see the small mole she has, just below her jawline. Her eyes are closed. Her head is on one side. Her body is covered across the chest with a sheet, but her abdomen below is exposed where there is an open wound in her stomach, being held back by clamps.

She cannot see the amulet around her neck and this makes her panic for a moment, until she is distracted by the activity below her.

Looking down, she sees the tops of the medics' heads, which are covered by pale blue caps; with surgical masks over their faces too, their sterile clothing makes them look like a uniformed army, sexless in the baggy clothes, each seeming to work in harmony with the other as they operate on her. They bend over her, one stepping aside as another performs a task; they are precise, unhurried, yet working with such care. Then there's a warning beep from a machine and a burst of tension from the team as they realise they need to act quickly. They move to restart her heart and she hears a shout. 'Clear!'

They all move away from her body in unison as if at a given signal; gloved hands, some smeared with her blood, pull away from her as electrodes are placed on her chest. Becky feels the jolt, even as she is suspended above them. She hears a machine that had been whining with one long, deep pulse suddenly resume a steady beat.

'She's back,' says one of the pale blue people, a woman to judge by her voice. The synchronised surgery continues.

Suspended high above them, Becky looks ahead and can see the digital clock on the wall telling her it is three fifty-eight. The operating theatre below is spartan but Becky is fascinated by the open wound in her abdomen; her eyes keep going back to it as she looks down at the doctors who are trying to save her. She can feel no pain at all. She feels disconnected. She can see dark blood being fed through a tube into her body alongside a drip. That machine is beeping loudly, rhythmically. One of the medics is monitoring her vital signs constantly. Becky can see that this is a man, she can see the black hairs on his thick wrist where the thin surgical gloves end.

Now Becky looks up and around at the room. She can see the air conditioning vent just beneath the ceiling. She is suspended just at the side of one of the strip lights illuminating the theatre below and she hears the electric whir of the fluorescent tube, sounding like a mosquito. She can sense the greater urgency and speed with which this group of people, unknown to her, are working. She can see the sweat on the brow of the older man who appears to be leading the team trying to save her life. A nurse leans over – she has grey streaks in her brown hair around her temples – and dabs his forehead.

Becky calmly watches, whilst wanting to move on and out of this room. She knows that she can. She feels calm, perfectly accepting the fact that a part of her, her physical body, is now separate and laid out below her. There is no sense of strangeness or panic. There is also no gravity to hold her now; she would be able to soar away. As she looks down on her physical self, the shell she has risen out of, she feels herself begin to rise higher, as if the very thought of moving can produce motion. Becky looks down at her body one more time, vulnerable, so vulnerable, and begins to move away from it. She feels as if her time here is done.

She soars.

A police car, siren wailing, rushed down Bloomsbury Way, past the junction with Museum Street. Bert Brookings turned away from it and looked in a shop window displaying kitchen equipment. The siren peaked in decibels and then faded in a matter of seconds, and he turned back again to walk down the A401.

He had slipped unseen into a side street and taken off the jacket with the hood and reversed it. Zipped up, any stains were hidden. His jeans were black, disguising the blood splatters well enough. He had removed the gloves, saturated with blood, and dropped them along with the Glock pistol, bought illegally from an East European in a backstreet pub in Merthyr Tydfil, into a bin in Bedford Square Gardens as he'd walked unhurriedly away from the Dominion and down Bloomsbury Street. He hadn't run from the scene of the shooting, just strolled away. No one had challenged him, because they were all staring at his handiwork.

Bert felt invincible. He had rid the world of Becky Moran, the unbeliever, the woman who destroyed his world. He had no thought for the other woman he fired at. She was screaming and simply had to be stopped. If Brookings had any regrets at all as he walked in a state of cautious ecstasy, adrenalin pumping through his body, it was that he hadn't shot Hugh Jolly's face off too. This was his revenge, his mission: to restore the Power of the Unicorn.

Whilst he had no thought of being hunted down (for he was indomitable) Bert was sly enough to make sure he was inconspicuous. The tattoos were covered. He was protected by his Astral Enchantment, a stellar army guiding him. He was riding the stars. The late Sunday afternoon traffic was steady on Bloomsbury Way. Brookings was less than a third of a mile from the Dominion Theatre and about two minutes' walk from the British Museum, very near to the room he rented as his London office. He was heading for St George's Church in Bloomsbury. Consecrated in 1730, it was an imposing landmark, despite being shadowed by a modern hotel.

Just another historic church in a city full of historic churches.

But it was not history that interested Bert Brookings. His purpose was far higher. He despised the literary tourists who visited the church because it was where the Victorian novelist Anthony Trollope was baptised. Brookings didn't know Trollope from tripe. As for the feminists and historians who visited on a pilgrimage to pay homage to the struggles of those who won votes for women, Bert would have laughed out loud. The funeral of the suffragette Emily Davison had taken place there after she had been hit by the king's horse during the 1913 Derby. A suicidal sacrifice to the cause. Waste of space, Brookings thought. And a waste of a good horse.

As for the admirers of early eighteenth-century architecture, visiting St George's to take in the imposing columned entrance with the grand sweep of stone steps, a small echo of the design of St Paul's Cathedral, Brookings would have been only too happy to tell them to get up the Brecon Beacons and look at some real nature, not man-made bricks and mortar. And anyone using this church to worship a so-called deity would have Brookings laughing with absolute derision.

However, a few visitors would share an interest with Brookings. They came to study the unusual and infamous spire, tucked behind the clean lines of the frontage, but not placed as the central feature at the entrance to the church. This spire was set well back at the rear of the church. It was also built slightly to the left, almost as if it were an architectural afterthought.

This church had obsessed Brookings. He had, unusually, taken the time to research it. It was the spire of St George's which drew him, ever since he had caught a glimpse of it while on a bus one afternoon. Church spires were usually symbols of man reaching high into the sky towards God in His Heaven. This one almost looked as if the architect thought that function entirely secondary to his man-made vision of worship. The pale stone frontage had a neoclassical air about it and the tall spire looked almost whimsical rather than intended to acknowledge the deity. It was decidedly off-centre. However, to assume that this church spire was insignificant would be a great mistake.

The spire was cast in stone and shaped like a pyramid as it reached upwards. At the very top, a statue of King George I – immortalised as St George – looked out over London. It was this steeple that Bert wanted, that he needed; the steeple was calling him. More specifically, it was the newly restored statues at the base of the pyramid steeple that were calling. That Sunday afternoon, scaffolding and sheeting surrounded the steeple where stonemasons were finishing off their expensive and detailed restoration work on four stone beasts, fighting over a royal coat of arms.

Heavy with symbolism, the statues reflected the religious politics of the early 1700s. Two countries, two faiths were at war: England shaped into two fierce lions, Scotland represented by two magnificent, mythical beasts, each with a twisted, long, golden horn, sharp, pointing upwards and glinting.

Unicorns.

As London hunted for a gunman, Bert Brookings was hunting for a unicorn, and he knew exactly where to find one.

Iris and Peter Moran were waiting for news. Dawn, the police liaison officer, was kind but not giving them any real information about what had happened. She reassured them that the search for the gunman was underway. Two cups of tea sat untouched on the Formica table. Iris had been mildly sedated and sat with her hands clasped together, staring at the floor. Peter had made it clear to Dawn that he didn't want anyone from Divine Diva anywhere near them.

Peter's anger, which had been bubbling for over a decade, now placed the blame for this, the possible murder of his only child, with Hugh Jolly – and saw it as a direct result of this pantomime of a career. Peter had made it clear down the years that he didn't want his daughter exploiting the vulnerable, that she should have had a decent career with decent people. He loved Becky, but someone had to be blamed for this tragedy – so horrific, so unthinkable. He was angry that Becky had ever been put in this situation and he wished that it were Hugh Jolly lying in that operating theatre, not his girl. He didn't believe this shooting was random. Otherwise, it made no sense. Iris rocked slightly in her chair, her eyes glassy. Peter didn't know what he would do, or how Iris would cope, if their only daughter died.

Sarah was still in the waiting room of Casualty, mobile phone in hand. Once Olly had a grip on dealing with the immediate demands of cancelling tonight's show, he would come down and wait with her. She saw some press activity outside. The online news sites were already reporting a shooting in central London outside the Dominion Theatre, but not naming the victims. There was a manhunt underway, but the Metropolitan Police had not yet made any statements.

Sarah couldn't raise Hugh at all. She hoped he wasn't swimming in vodka. All she could do was wait. She bit her lip, her anxiety and shock making her want to run through the hospital, shouting Becky's name. It was highly unlikely that Lulu LaBelle had survived. She had been shot point blank in the head, while Becky's wound was in her abdomen, and Sarah still had her blood on her clothes, despite the clean-up attempt.

The reception area of A&E was busy with people milling around. A child was screaming. Sarah looked up to see a police officer walking towards her. She was immediately afraid that this young man would gently lead her away and tell her that Becky Moran was dead, so she sat, numb with terror, as he approached.

'Sarah Jones?' he asked. Sarah nodded, tears in her eyes. 'Can we get a witness statement from you about what you saw at the Dominion?'

Sarah stood up. 'How is she – Becky? What about Lulu LaBelle?' The officer indicated that she should follow him. 'Is Becky okay?' Sarah was now frantic. She was led to a quiet room, right inside the hospital.

Aiden O'Conner was in the Cube. The Prime Minister had been into the studios for the Politics Show earlier that morning. Aiden always made a point of being in the studio area when the PM arrived, shaking hands and exchanging a word or two with his press officer and minder. He wanted to make sure he got his invitation to the Christmas drinks reception at 10 Downing Street. The bow tie today was a lime green, hand-tied construction. Aiden had watched the interview as it was broadcast, then he'd escaped back upstairs to his executive suite to fire off some succinct orders by email before going for a late lunch, to be followed by a stroll. Soon he would go to see Becky Moran on stage at the Dominion. He'd slipped his mobile phone into the pocket of his checked jacket, making sure it was on silent. After all, even masters of the universe needed time out. He left the Cube, thinking about Becky Moran's legs.

Hugh, with Olly's help, had issued instructions to the theatre for a press statement simply saying that *'With deep regret and sincere apologies, and due to unforeseen circumstances, tonight's Evening with Becky Moran, the Cambridge Medium will be postponed.'* Either a full refund or exchange of tickets would be available. Hugh's eyes were bloodshot, and his hands were unsteady, but he'd drunk no more vodka that afternoon. The police had said they would be issuing a statement shortly and had advised Hugh not to speak to any reporters until it was clear who they were looking for and, of course, when there was any news from the hospital. The police also told Hugh that Becky's parents had made it clear that no one from Divine Diva was welcome anywhere near them for the foreseeable future. As the gunman was still at large, the police would take Hugh and Olly down to the hospital to wait for news of Becky.

Hugh thought he would never forget the faces of Becky's parents as they saw the bloodstains on Tottenham Court Road and realised that their daughter had been shot. He told Olly this, tears in his eyes, saying he knew that they blamed him. They agreed that it sounded as if the shooter fitted Bert Brookings's description.

'Why would he want to shoot Becky? And that LaBelle woman – she didn't even know him,' said Olly, as they watched the sound and light crew de-rig the theatre. Everyone was in shock.

'Wrong place, wrong time,' murmured Hugh, speculating about Lulu. 'Brookings must have lost it and come looking for Becky. Christ.' He longed for a drink but knew he had to remain sober now. Both men were aware they may be Brookings's next targets after restraining and hauling him away from Becky in the studio.

'Do you remember that Becky said something about some sort of dark entity attached to Brookings before he went for her?' Olly was thinking back to that night in the Cube. 'I thought she was just making it up. What if she wasn't?'

Hugh nodded. They were anxious to get to University College Hospital now and the police escort got the two men out of the Dominion, avoiding the news crews and journalists.

As the police car drove away with lights flashing and siren wailing, Olly felt a deep sadness. He remembered seeing Becky on his camera monitor when they'd been filming outside the Lancaster bomber. She'd looked beautiful, like a wraith, with those grey eyes. He very much wanted Becky back, smoothing her red hair with one hand and then amazing him with what she did next.

Olly knew that time may well have passed.

Becky is suspended, weightless. No longer looking down at her body, shattered and bleeding, she is floating. All around her is a bright, warm light. There is no water around her, but the sensation is like being in a vast ocean, being rolled gently by an unseen current. She smells ozone, sharp and clean. Becky feels that she could slowly dissolve, meld into this buoyancy. All her memories, her senses, her life force could drift into this glorious deep, becoming a part of it, embracing it. She stretches out her arms, rocking slowly, feeling safe and ready to give way, to willingly allow this billowing ether to lap over her head and complete a journey that she is now only just realising is nearly done. She closes her eyes and it feels like an act of surrender.

Becky is peaceful and safe. She will sink into this softness, become part of it and dissolve into it. The light is welcoming, the air surrounding her feels gentle, fragrant, and enveloping.

But the rocking motion now becomes less soothing and Becky is being buffeted by the unseen current. There is a forceful tug that does not want her to be absorbed; it is as though this unseen ocean is rejecting her. Far from allowing her weight to slip down, the surge is pushing her away. She is being carried on a swell, a breaker, almost as though this space is expelling her. The sensation is a subtle yet firm rejection. Becky feels an acute sadness; she had been so comforted.

The tug becomes a pull. The movement is no longer benign. The unseen ocean swells, heaving with huge waves of slow, forceful power. Becky feels tipped upwards and sideways as the mass around her begins to swirl and bubble. The sensation is one of being pulled towards a force that is forming, circling like whirls of a maelstrom in concentric circles of energy, widening as she is dragged towards it, a cone of dark space wrapped within it that descends into blackness. She feels herself being thrown into that vortex, that cyclone quickly sucking at her, and she is spinning like a pin on a magnet that has no north point, no anchor, no order.

Streams of dark air fly like ribbons all around Becky, twisting and wrapping themselves around her as this power spins her away from the surface, away from that peace, away from comfort. She is dizzy with the speed and the force, disorientated and very afraid. The whirlpool now begins to slow, winding down, and Becky can hear her name being shouted over the noise of the swirling forces. Her name is being called repeatedly, demanding her attention. Then everything, at last, becomes calm, the voice becomes less demanding, less urgent.

As she opens her eyes, dizzy and fighting for balance in the darkness, her senses struggling to adjust, she hears it clearly.

'Becky...' That familiar low, whispering voice. 'We are here.'

Becky cannot move.

There is no hellish choir now, no vibration; this is a simple immersion in total darkness. She feels cold, the seeping coldness that comes from ancient stone, damp, icy, relentless. Becky is in a compressed wrap of atmosphere so dense that light would struggle to penetrate it. The barrier of blackness is moulded around her eyes, binding her limbs, rendering around her flesh so she is wrapped within folds and layers as if she were a mummy, prepared for an eternity in a gilded box with her organs cut out and placed into clay jars, her brain removed slowly through her septum. But there are no scented oils, nothing to anoint her. Her existence has been silenced in a shroud for eternity.

Now Becky can hear a steady, swooping noise. There's a whoosh of air as if a huge, dark, feathered wing is slicing through that deeper darkness, propelling itself in an unseen motion. She hears it again. She is disorientated, the blackness pressing on her eyes like lead pennies meant to close her corpse eyelids for eternity; whatever is making that sound cannot be seen. There is no displacement of air as she hears that sweeping sound again. In her imagination, Becky sees a huge demonic creature. This is no angel, but a creature with a huge wingspan, twisted and demonic, with a red gash of a mouth, flying into her darkness.

In desperation, Becky realises that her absorption in this obscure vacuum will not allow her to hide. Why would it? Whatever is making that sound also created this sepulchre and that creator stands somewhere nearby, waiting. Becky is the object that has been entrapped.

Something soft now touches her face.

Then there's that smell, so familiar, rotting, sweet, that stench of decay, becoming stronger as something traces the line of her cheek. It is almost a caress. Like a black feather, the ethereal tip being stroked downwards on her skin, tracing her jawline, sweeping over her neck. Becky wants to scream out, repulsed by a violation so intimate and so knowing, but she has no voice. The darkness binds her completely. She tries to move, struggling to free herself before that unknown presence can cover her, absorb her, eradicate her in this tomb it has created. But she cannot even turn her face away.

Then the touch is withdrawn. There is nothing. No sound, no stench, no air. She simply lies wrapped in the black obscurity of this place.

'We are here,' the voice whispers in her ear. 'You are ours now.'

Peter stood up as the medics came into the waiting room – an older man who looked tired and a woman with greying brown hair. He stared at their hands, knowing that they'd been operating on his little girl. Iris sat in her chair, her eyes fixed on their hands, her own clenched tightly together.

The surgeon introduced himself to Peter and invited him to sit down. Peter refused; he just asked, simply and quietly, whether Becky was dead.

'She is in a coma,' the doctor answered. Iris slumped forward, and Dawn went over to her, held her up and soothed her gently. 'We have removed the bullet. She has lost her spleen and the blood loss was extensive, I'm afraid. We had to restart her heart in theatre. Your daughter is on life support and we shall know in the next few hours if she will survive. I am sorry I cannot be more optimistic than that. We have done our best and she is young, strong, and healthy. She was very lucky that the bullet missed the other vital organs.'

'I want to see her.'

'Yes, of course. The intensive care team are with her and we'll take you and your wife to her as soon as we can.' Then the surgeon looked sharply at Peter Moran. 'Do you have a faith?'

'Yes,' answered Peter.

'May I suggest you pray for her? Everything will help.'

Iris was rocking, Dawn holding her with her arms on her shoulders. 'Thank you, thank you,' Iris said quietly.

'I do the surgery,' said the doctor. 'Let's hope a higher force can do the rest.'

The medics left after repeating that a nurse would come shortly and take them to Becky in intensive care. Peter looked at the door as it closed behind them. He bowed his head and began to pray.

A vibration begins to thrum through Becky's body. As if some permission has been given, the darkness before her eyes becomes an opaque light, almost as though she is viewing the world from underwater where scum, filth, and membranous embryos cluster just below the surface, a sulphurous light filtering through the thick atmosphere.

Becky can see now. Her immediate instinct is to cover her face, to block her sight, to protect herself. Hovering above her, emerging out of that gloom, being hewn out of the dense blackness, is a deep splurge of crimson as a shape opens up out of the dark air like a flower unfurling in front of her, casting aside shards of thick, textured dark matter as it billows and grows, pulsing, red and hungry, greedily towards her. The teeth emerge like venomous stamens in the carnivorous petals. Becky feels a droplet of drool, toxic saliva, fall on her face. She closes her eyes and prays for death.

As the redness approaches to cover her, Becky Moran realises she is already dead.

CHAPTER SEVENTEEN

Bert Brookings stood before St George's, the church with the most peculiar spire in England. The nearby street was quiet, the traffic light, and worshippers and tourists were leaving Bloomsbury on this late Sunday afternoon in central London. Londoners were heading back to the suburbs to prepare for a new working week. Afternoon tea was being served in the modern hotel that nudged this much older church building. Anyone standing outside the hotel could look into the dining area and see the white tablecloths on small, round tables, and the tiered plates of delicate sandwiches and scones. Tea was being poured from white teapots into china cups and guests were spooning cream and jam in a heap alongside the cakes.

But Brookings, riding an astral plane all of his own, was not interested in tea. He flexed his back and the elaborate unicorn tattoo galloped under his bloodstained shirt. He was filled with the Power of the Unicorn, his insanity creating his own world, his purpose clear. He must reach the unicorn and ride the mythical beast that guided his way, his path to invincibility, his astral ministry, his pathway to the stars. Once he reached the unicorn, the stars and the galaxies would be his. Bert's hands flexed in anticipation, the muscles playing under the inked skin of his arms. He felt as if his humanity had been subsumed by the power emanating from the twin unicorns at the base of the church spire. All he had to do was reach them, climb them, ride them, and he would become one with the stars and master of his own universe. He would merge into the galaxy and return to Earth all-conquering.

Brookings looked up. The scaffolding reached to the top of the spire, built in levels, the large metal bolts holding the structure together, with worn wooden boards lining each platform. This section of the church was wrapped in polythene, the opaque, thick plastic flapping slightly in the late afternoon breeze. Brookings saw the contractor's sign, 'Raine Master Stonemasons of London', attached to the scaffolding, advertising the firm undertaking the restoration. But no one was working this Sunday afternoon. Bert had slipped through central London, anonymous and bloodstained. His natural cunning and sense of invisibility, his mind engrossed in his own insane world, had allowed him to walk right through the manhunt for a killer.

He was energised by the shooting of Becky Moran. He felt neither remorse nor fear. Why should he when the completion of his journey to the astral planes, becoming one with the unicorn and achieving galactic dominance, was now just minutes away? Brookings stepped towards the struts of the scaffolding that surrounded the base of the building. He parted the edges of the polythene tarpaulin and slipped inside. He began to climb, unseen, up towards the base of the spire that sat atop this off-centre addition to the old, historic church. His heart beat slightly faster as he saw the golden spike of one of the unicorns, sitting waiting for him high above the ground.

Olly and Hugh sat in a small room at University College Hospital, comforting Sarah, as a police officer explained that they were under police protection while they waited for news and until the gunman was found, but that Becky's parents refused to see anyone from Divine Diva. Hugh needed to reach for his hipflask; Olly was staring out of a grimy window, pale with shock; Sarah was crying, telling Hugh she needed to see Becky. All the police would say was that Becky was in theatre. No, said the young officer, there was no news of the search for the gunman. He didn't know anything about the other woman who was shot. Sarah repeated that she felt guilty she hadn't gone with Becky to meet Lulu LaBelle.

'I didn't like her, that Lulu,' she explained to Hugh. 'But she didn't deserve this. If I'd been there, I would have done something. I could have saved Becky.' Sarah's eyes were red from crying. Hugh shook his head and put his arm around her, ignoring the waft of mothballs for once.

'No one could have seen this happening, Sarah. Even Becky didn't know.'

Olly looked at them, a flash of anger on his face. 'If you had all just stuck with the fact that Becky never had a gift – this bloody nonsense about the dead talking – she may be alive now. We are all to blame. All of us.'

Hugh shook his head. 'No, Olly. Becky did have something and all we did was give that an outlet. We can't be blamed for the actions of some tattooed Welsh lunatic. If any of us had guessed what he may do – well, don't you think we'd have stopped it?'

'What?' said Olly. 'You're saying you would never have let him near Becky? Him with all his advertising revenue? He was clearly deluded yet you gave him the airtime, you exposed Becky to him, not to mention all the other wackjobs. I blame you, Hugh. And I blame myself.'

Olly stood up and began to pace the small room. Sarah wept. Hugh glared at Olly, his expression telling him to be quiet.

They waited for news.

Peter and Iris Moran were taken to the ICU. A nurse called Sharon had come into their waiting room, her face sympathetic, and Iris had begun to cry as she entered. Peter had stood up, his back straight, waiting to hear the worst. Sharon had smiled and introduced herself and then said that they could see Becky now. Peter's entire body had slumped with relief. Dawn went to get an update on the hunt for the gunman.

As they walked down the corridor to the lifts, Sharon explained that they must not be alarmed at how Becky looked, that she was receiving the best possible care, and that they should talk to her. Coma victims could still hear and having her mum and dad at her bedside could help. She reassured them that the ICU was state of the art and that one nurse would be with Becky constantly, monitoring her physical state.

'Do we need to be disinfected?' asked Iris, looking at one of the hand sanitising units that were everywhere, attached to the walls and by every door. Peter squeezed his wife's arm in reassurance.

'Just disinfect your hands, please,' Sharon answered. 'We'll give you a plastic gown to wear over your clothes.'

Inside, Becky was lying on a bed that seemed far too big for her. Peter looked from the tubes attached to his daughter's body to the nearby flashing computer screens, signalling Becky's vital signs. Her small, fragile body was outlined under the white sheets and all he could see of her was her pale face and a few strands of her red hair, tucked away under a cap. Peter thought she looked very, very young. Iris made a small moaning sound as she looked at her child, prone in a hospital bed, her life in the balance.

Peter turned to Iris before they reached the bedside.

'Listen to me,' he said gently, his hands on his wife's shoulders. 'We may never have to do anything so hard, so shocking, ever again in our lives, Iris. But Becky needs us now, to hear us, to know we are here. Can you do that? For her? For us?' Iris's eyes went from Peter's face to her daughter, lying in that bed; then she looked back at Peter, her own face old and tired.

'Yes,' was the simple, quiet answer. Iris took a deep breath and stepped towards her daughter. Peter followed.

The ICU nurse sat near the foot of the bed on a high stool, with notes spread out in front of him on a table. He looked up and smiled as Peter approached the bed. 'Hello, I am Nigel,' he said and indicated that Peter and Iris should sit at the two chairs at the side of the bed. Peter had been told that the nurse's entire job was to keep Becky alive. Nigel was slim and young, his uniform a crisp white against the black of his skin. His smile was warm.

'Please talk to her, she may well hear you. Tell her anything you think she needs to know. Keep telling her. Anything at all.'

'Can I touch her?' Iris asked Nigel as she sat in the chair to the left-hand side. He nodded. Iris took her daughter's hand, holding her fingertips away from the drip attached to a vein in Becky's hand. Peter sat opposite, tears in his eyes, looking at this vulnerable, small human being – his only child. Becky looked asleep. Instantly, he was reminded of how he would read to her when she was small, and she would drift away as he finished the story, curled and safe and warm in her bed, soothed by the sound of his voice. He took her other hand.

'Becky, it's Dad, love,' he said quietly. 'We are with you.'

Nigel looked up from his charts.

'Yes, just talk to her. Her body has endured a tremendous shock. The coma is a way of shutting down so that healing can begin. She lost a great deal of blood, but the surgical team have removed the bullet, as well as her spleen. They had to restart her heart too, which means that her brain… You see, oxygen deficiency affects the neurons of the cerebral cortex and the hippocampus, so…' Nigel paused. 'But we have to be prepared for the possibility of some brain damage,' he continued. It was his job. 'Still, she may recover completely, if we help her now. It's just vital that you talk to her because she can hear you.'

'Becky was wearing this,' said Nigel, handing Iris a small plastic bag containing an obsidian crystal, jet black with white flecks in the shape of a half-moon, on a silver chain. 'You should keep it safe – we'll give you a receipt form to sign for it.'

'She never wore any jewellery,' Iris said to Peter. 'Do you think this was important to her?'

Peter had no idea. It had struck him in the last three hours that there was much about his daughter he didn't know. He took the plastic bag from his wife, opened it and tipped the black amulet out. It felt warm and comfortable in the palm of his hand.

'It may well have been. I've never known her to wear so much as an earring.' Peter took Becky's other hand and placed the amulet in her palm, closing her fingers around it. 'There you go, Becky. It's back with you. Come on, love, Mum and Dad are here too. We're with you. Fight, Becky, come back to us.' With tears in his eyes, he closed his hand around his daughter's fist, the amulet clasped within her fingers, and looked at his wife, who was stroking Becky's other hand. 'Talk to her, Iris.'

A flash of light, a strobe of blue-white intensity, exploding, harsh and relentless in front of that crimson and black. A beacon sliver of pure white light ruptures the blackness for a split second. It is as if a flashlight of huge intensity has ripped through the textured darkness, leaving a ghost-like image of vivid bright streaks. The crimson, unfurling mass hangs suspended as if its progress, that obscene birth out of the blackness, has been pushed back, halted. The waves of crimson, the acid drool, that mouth hovering so close, hungry to absorb, to devour, seem frozen.

Then the waves of light begin to fade and some force, some dark energy that is feeding into the crimson, begins to gather once more as if the light were irrelevant and it is only darkness that powers this place. That unfurling redness begins to undulate once more, unfurling in a deadly unity with the black vacuum.

Becky knows that she will be sucked into that darkness. Some part of her mind remembers all the people she fooled into thinking she could talk to the dead. She remembers their vulnerability. This is her punishment, this death, this crimson mouth taking her. Her sorrow and regret build as terror develops, soaking her soul, and she cries out a silent prayer for forgiveness as she longs for the oblivion of death and an end to this, all of it. She knows she has to atone. She can taste her mortality and her dread is now absorbed by a wish that the end is quick. Becky Moran will cease. She surrenders to the darkness.

Flash.

Brighter, whiter, more powerful. This time, the light bathes the darkness entirely. Its intensity pushes into the blackness, ending it, a single strobe of energy both exploding the vacuum and tearing at the textured, heavy atmosphere, shards of light ripping into the black fabric in a star-shaped explosion. There follows a prism of rainbow-hued sparkling beams shooting through the vacuum, claiming the space and bringing in a passage of air and clarity.

As the brightness fades, Becky can now see pinpricks of light above her. It is as if she is looking up at the sky as night emerges and the stars begin to be visible, the glow touching her from light years away. There is no recognisable constellation here, just a twinkling swathe of small lights, white and gently flickering. The ripped fabric of the blackness hangs above her like a torn curtain, the crimson now diminished to a fading red mass, the colour of rotting meat, as if it were being pulled backwards by a force in retreat, though Becky can still feel the burn of the drops from that deadly maw dripping onto her face.

And it has not given up yet. To her dismay, the flickering pinpoints of light begin to fade and the black hole above her deepens. Becky can hear and feel the air around her begin to undulate again with that thrum, thrum, thrum. She lies suspended and unable to move, her eyes still registering the streaks of the bright light imprinted on her retinae as the deep well of darkness begins to gather in intensity once more, becoming more defined, rebuilding, gathering to attack and eject its crimson, spew it out to cover her and take her into its depths.

She is frozen, her soul in the hands of light and dark.

Then, as if someone has thrown a great switch, Becky's world and the space around her, under her, and covering her, bursts into a crystal whiteness, a brightness of such intensity that it blinds her, swaddles her, infuses her, blasts into her skin and envelops her every cell. She rises to the light. Becky has become the light itself, a power source rejecting and expelling the darkness. She feels the prism wrap around her and, as her eyes adjust, Becky thinks she can see the light begin to take shape in the forms of entities very much like the spirits she has been seeing from the Other Side, coming towards her, ready to take her towards the source of the light. Becky yearns to be with them as their energy reaches out to her. They begin to move towards her, protecting her as the shards of blackness recede, blasted by the light.

At last, Becky feels peace. She reaches out towards the figures emerging in the dappled crystal arcs and realises that she is moving towards her salvation. One shimmering figure, wrapped in this gauze of light, is leading her, drawing her, as if to guide her away from the dark. She feels as though she is being pulled by some invisible gossamer thread towards this shape, subtle and filled with brightness. If her existence is to be extinguished, she feels no more fear. She moves on, pulled by that invisible thread.

Bert Brookings was climbing towards the unicorns. The climb had little to do with scaling the metal poles of the scaffolding. He was moving across the cosmos, scaling the stars to where his salvation lay with the waiting creatures and their spiralling, golden horns. He could sense them, crouched and waiting. When Bert reached them, their stone façade would be cast aside, and they would ride the universe together.

The polythene tarpaulin buffered against the scaffolding with a dull slapping sound. Bert's climb was hidden from anyone below; he scaled the levels easily, his physical body well able to climb higher and higher. He passed the clock tower, the hands on its black face and golden numerals stopped during the renovation.

Upwards, past the colonnades that surrounded the final layer, an echo of the neoclassical design of the church front.

Bert reached the small platform where the stepped, pyramidal spire began, and the four corners sloped upwards to the pinnacle. The two lions and the two unicorns were ornately carved, hewn out of pale stone. Each beast was clinging to the base of the pyramid, straddling the rising edges of the stepped spire. The lions were roaring face down, their tails sweeping up the spire's rise; the unicorns faced upwards, their horns raised towards the sky.

Bert stood, breathing heavily, on the narrow wooden platform the restorers had placed beneath the sculptures. He just had to sit on the back of one of the unicorns so that the astral power could carry them both away. There was no scaffolding above this platform, so Bert would have to climb the pyramid steps of the spire and lower himself down onto the beast. He was filled with awe and anticipation at the sight of his chosen unicorn. He removed his bloodstained jacket and ripped off the bloody t-shirt so that his body art was in full view, in honour of the creature. He flexed the muscles across his back and the tattoo followed the movement, rippling in the sheen of sweat on his flesh.

He bowed his head in deference to the unicorns and moved towards the spire.

Hugh Jolly felt his mobile phone vibrating in his Gucci jacket. There were bloodstains on the sleeve, Becky's blood. His phone was switched to silent because newspaper and other journalists kept calling for an update, a quote, a statement. Hugh, for once, was ignoring them all. He took his arm from around Sarah, glanced at Olly, who hadn't spoken a word since his outburst, and retrieved the phone. It was Aiden O'Conner. He let it go to voicemail. The last thing Hugh needed was that Irishman screaming that he wanted an exclusive about Becky. He could wait.

O'Conner had been totally unaware of the events of that Sunday afternoon. His phone had been on silent and, after lunch, he had made his way down Oxford Street to look at bow ties in

Selfridges on his way to the Dominion. His plan was to have a drink before he took his seat in the box at the theatre, which Divine Diva had arranged for him. He was looking forward to admiring Becky Moran doing whatever she did on stage. He thought he would go and see her afterwards and offer to take her to Annabel's in Berkley Square.

As Aiden had turned into Tottenham Court Road, he'd seen the blue police tape and the cordon of uniformed officers and he could hear the wail of the sirens. He'd called his newsroom. He'd listened, amidst the chaos, to the news that two women had been shot outside the theatre and one of them was Becky Moran, although the police had released no statement. No one could reach Hugh Jolly; in fact, Olly Harvey had even blanked the Voice of Britain reporter waiting earlier in the press scrum outside.

O'Conner was incredulous that Becky had been shot. His mind went back to the last time he had seen her at the Cube, in that slinky black dress with that fall of red hair. O'Conner ran through in his mind who may be responsible. Was it terror, a radicalised Islamist? Unlikely. A raving born-again Christian, an evangelical who thought that what Becky did was the work of the devil? Possibly. Or just some unknown nutter with a gun? Aiden had to admit to himself that the thought of Becky being dead was deeply shocking. He'd run his hand over his belly, watching the aftermath of the crime playing out in front of him, and sighed.

Then the hard-nosed journalist had begun to take over. O'Conner realised he was furious that this was a big story his radio station should have the inside track on; then he'd calculated the impact of one of his presenters being shot and what that publicity would do. He'd put out his hand to hail a cab to get back to the Cube. He felt a small pang of shame that he'd been fantasising about Becky Moran's legs, but his instinct turned towards managing this story and making sure he had the lead. The possibility that Becky may be dead had become just another element in breaking news.

O'Conner straightened the lime green bow tie and pressed the number on his phone for Hugh Jolly.

Bert Brookings was well away on his astral plane. He was climbing a galaxy, ascending high into the universe, surrounded by spinning stars and planets, and all he had to do was climb a little higher up the pyramidal spire to harness the Power of the Unicorn. Then he would be reborn. He would become truly invincible.

The stone spire was a stepped pyramid as it rose to its pinnacle. Bert just needed to climb up a few metres then descend, triumphant, onto the back of the stone unicorn. He had to conquer the beast by descending onto its back, one dominant force astride another. He looked at the sharp, gilded, twisted horn – the creature was trembling with anticipation for Bert to set it free.

He put one foot on the stepped stone, his powerful hands gripping a higher ledge. His inked arms strained to hold on; the steps were narrow. He climbed cautiously but was grinning with triumph; he was just seconds away – he would rise above the unicorn and then manoeuvre his body to sit on its back. He edged sideways, looking down to make sure he was in the correct position.

'Power to the unicorn!' he shouted, his hand rising in a fist salute. And then he felt his balance shift; his foot jerked away from the stone step, and his other hand, still gripping the narrow ledge, slipped. He was falling, falling, his body arching backwards, then downwards to reach the upward, twisted, golden horn of the unicorn. Sharp and long, it impaled him through the heart. He was one with the unicorn.

Bert's body twitched. The tip of the horn had lanced through his back, slicing into the inked pretender and pushing out through his powerful chest. Blood spurted out, pouring down, soaking the stone unicorn and turning it a deep shade of crimson.

The blood dripped onto the wooden platform, winding its way to the metal scaffolding, and then slowly ran down the tarpaulin, down, down, towards the earth below.

Becky is surrounded by a soft, white light.

It is as if someone has put a soft, silk shawl over a Tiffany lamp so that the light source is obscured but the intricate pieces of coloured glass throw a spectrum of colour, so delicate, all around her. She can see the light forming into shapes, almost solid yet iridescent shapes that look human; there are many of them, emerging out of the light and standing near to her. The shape undulating with more light than the others, a brighter glimmer, is the entity that Becky wants to be near.

She feels no fear now, just a warmth and comfort. There is a familiarity about them too, these spirits who have come to her. They seem to float nearby, entranced by the fact she is with them where they are, whatever place this is that they inhabit. They can see her, these energies made of light and substance, existing in this level of ethereal illumination. Becky wants to thank them for driving away the dark. She feels a strong urge to step forward and touch them, to float in this softly focused world, to melt into their space. To be absorbed by their soft light.

The figures form a circle around her. Becky is reminded of that sphere, that glass bubble filled with the white mist she had yearned to see again; she believes these white shadows were in that glass globe, swirling and gentle. A clear, blue light now rims the circle, never-ending, buoyant, cupping the whiteness, and Becky is now in the centre. As she turns full circle, it is like a carousel of soft mist and blue infinity. There is no solid mass to these wispy figures, but she can see that they are waving, slowly, and a sense of sadness begins to build. Becky doesn't want to leave this protected circle, not even to see more of the space beyond this pocket of lustrous, shimmering vapour. She wants to step forward and join their circle, to be absorbed by them, but they are moving backwards, outwards, breaking away from one another as a vapour trail leads away, fading into the hazy blue.

They are sending her away. They are sending her back.

That one shape, amorphous but dominant, has broken the circle. The gleam of this shape rises above the others, which fade, melting into the blue. The aurora swirls and the misty, pearly shape radiates light.

And Becky realises that she has to choose: to meld into the mist, float after those energies and become one of them, or to move towards that vapour trail now forming a pathway back to her life. The spectre of radiant light hovers nearby, silently offering Becky a way forward – onto that trail of vapour surrounded by the icy blue, or she could take a step back into the ethereal light, join them. The choice is hers. There is no sense of fear or urgency. The way back into the circle is welcoming, the need to be part of that white energy is strong. And as Becky turns one way and then the other, she is aware that her humanity, her life force, her being, is waiting beyond the blue. For a split second, a sweep of the second hand on a clock, less than a heartbeat, her energy seems drawn towards the milky, swirling mist that will welcome her.

Her desire for life, now that she knows what waits for her when that life is over, the need to live, to be, makes her turn towards the pathway.

As Becky moves towards the trail, delicate and soft with mist, the white begins to fade, and she can see and sense the spectres releasing her. She moves on, aware of a crystal shower of light creating an arch overhead. The figure of white vapour appears to nod and wave her away as Becky floats, gently, into that icy blue haze.

That feeling of floating now becomes overtaken by a cascade of intense colours swirling around her, then there's a swift drop, a sliding motion that takes her away from the blue with disorientating speed. Becky's feeling of weightlessness and serenity is being replaced by a physical wrap of pressure. She is being enclosed by a denser, thicker atmosphere and she can feel the pull of gravity, a heaviness, a feeling of the earth rushing up to meet her as if she were freefalling from a great height. Becky braces herself for the impact, afraid that the force of smashing into the ground will shatter her, is powerless to stop the incredibly fast, blurred skim of air and friction delivering her back into her physical self. The jarring, splintering explosion of pain fills her. She feels her heart beating hard as she inhales sharply.

In the ICU bed, with her parents clasping her hands, the amulet still in her enclosed fist, Becky Moran opens her eyes.

CHAPTER EIGHTEEN

AFTERWORD

Becky's recovery time was long. She spent another two weeks in ICU with Nigel and the team nursing her. Then she had to take her first steps, undergo daily physiotherapy, and endure weeks of heavy-duty painkillers. Becky was then ordered to rest for months. Every day she felt more positive, her experience gave her the strength to get better. What she had endured gave her hope and she felt protected, saved, and now Becky was grateful for this gift of connecting with the dead. The dead had saved her. She knew that. She also knew that she had been saved for a reason.

Ironically, her fame was now assured. She became known as 'the Cambridge Medium Who Came Back from the Dead', a sobriquet the *Daily Mail* loved.

As soon as she was able, Hugh had organised interviews and her face was plastered throughout the media. She told the story of what had happened after she was gunned down and the masses loved it. It was as if she were assuring them that death was not the end. Those of faith believed that their chosen deity existed; it was just a little bit more proof, or at least evidence, feeding that faith. Those of science had their own explanations. These did not include God.

But Becky never fully told the story of the dark force that had emerged before she was shot, and then came for her again while she was in her coma. She preferred to dwell on the light. She felt that this was why she had returned, to give hope. It was up to others to interpret what it meant. Becky knew that what she had experienced after Brookings shot her was difficult to explain, yet it was as real to her as the scar in her abdomen from the surgery that had saved her life.

She had recognised the surgeon when he came to see her. She had also told her ICU nurse Nigel about what had happened while she was unconscious, but Nigel had responded that what she was describing was 'quite common'. Near-death experiences were 'interesting', but scientists knew that it was just how the brain reacted when the body suffered severe trauma and a lack of oxygen to the cerebral cortex when the heart stopped. When Becky had then told Nigel, in great detail, about being out of her body and hovering over the operating table in theatre, and subsequently recognising the surgeon and the medical team who had saved her life, even Nigel was surprised. However, he merely soothed her, telling her to focus on getting better and to be thankful she survived. Becky could see a figure shimmering next to Nigel, his mother who had passed years before, and she told Becky that her boy was a nurse first and foremost. Becky told Nigel his mum was with him and described her. But Nigel just smiled, as if Becky needed more painkillers or it was the morphine talking.

Divine Diva had suspended *Medium Wave* until Becky was ready to return to work, and her parents had taken her back to Leeds to convalesce. She was home.

Because she was still very weak, Becky had not been able to go to Lulu LaBelle's funeral, but Hugh, Olly, and Sarah went. Sarah wore a black onesie with a glitter beret. There were few mourners and certainly, unfortunately, no one famous. The saddest thing was that the only thing Lulu would be remembered for was being shot dead instead of Becky Moran. Hugh had needed a lot of vodkas that day. Even the shock of what had happened to Becky had not made him rethink his addiction to alcohol.

Sarah had arrived to see Becky as soon as she was out of the ICU and had held her hand for a long time, beaming with joy that her friend was going to be all right.

Becky learned later that she had been in a coma for a week, with her parents at her side the whole time. Aiden O'Conner had sent a huge bunch of yellow roses with a shamrock as soon as she recovered consciousness. There was a kiss on the Get Well Soon card. Becky had smiled. The very married Frenchman, François Bertrand, whom she had met just minutes before she was shot, had sent an orchid and a message saying that he hoped to see Becky soon. Iris sniffed at the French name.

'Keep away from foreigners, Becky. They can't be trusted,' she had warned.

Eventually, Hugh had come to see her in Leeds, enduring Peter's cold rage and Iris's vol-au-vents. Hugh and Peter had gone into the living room, where Peter vented his rage at Hugh. Making sure the door was closed so that Becky couldn't hear, Peter accused Hugh of pimping his daughter for money, of peddling an act of fraud and manipulating the grief of others. Peter told Hugh that he despised him, that he had taken a bright and lovely girl and turned her into a freak show, a supernatural construct of the lowest order; and whilst Hugh hadn't actually fired that gun, he might as well have attempted to murder her. Peter made it clear that he loathed everything Hugh stood for.

Hugh took it all, assured Peter that he had accused himself of everything Peter was accusing him of and that he was sorry. Then he had swept back his floppy hair and told Peter the story of Becky seeing his own father in his London flat and assured him that whatever Becky had, it was real. That took some courage and Peter looked on the point of hitting him. Their conversation took over two hours and, when it was over, the men reluctantly shook hands and agreed that the future – whether or not to continue with the construction that was Becky Moran – would be Becky's choice entirely and that Hugh would not interfere with that decision.

Peter had emerged from the living room ashen-faced and gone to see Becky, hoping she would decide not to renew any claims of being a medium. His daughter had just looked away and said she may not have a choice.

They had found Brookings's body the morning after he fell from the spire. The stonemason was now in counselling for post-traumatic stress disorder. He told his wife he had found Brookings 'skewered like a kebab' on one of the unicorns and he had never seen so much blood.

The police later confirmed that Brookings had been the gunman and the case was closed. There were no mourners at his cremation. But St George's Church in Bloomsbury was now even more famous for its peculiar spire.

On a beautiful early May afternoon, Becky Moran made her way to the Cube.

Medium Wave was now back on the air every Friday night, its return much publicised. Becky now felt a much stronger connection with the spirits; she saw them more clearly and they came to her constantly, but she had learned to deflect their attention with an imagined aura of white light and they got the message. There had been no more encounters with that darkness and crimson. Becky felt wiped clean.

Aiden made sure that The Voice of Britain had the first interview with Becky. Becky's picture now adorned the upper floor of the Cube, her red hair and off-the-shoulder black dress staring out over Covent Garden. She had a book deal and filming would resume shortly for the television pilot.

Becky walked to Covent Garden, getting off the Tube at Oxford Circus so that she could enjoy the day. She was back in her signature dress and her red-soled Louboutins. She stopped off at Patisserie Valerie in Soho for a cup of tea, enjoying the freedom and enjoying being alive. No spirits appeared this afternoon. Becky sipped her tea and watched as a child stared in awe at the rows of French cakes, unsure which one to select. There was a look of wonderment in the little boy's eyes as his mother urged him to hurry up; she smiled as he pointed at a macaroon, bright pink and the size of a saucer.

Sarah would be meeting Becky in Reception at the Cube, and then Becky and Olly would go through the notes for the radio show this evening. She looked down at the notes she'd been working on and felt that her life really had begun again.

Olly had spent the last three months working as a producer for a cable TV show called *Slappers on Tour*, a series following young women on their hen nights, mainly in Ibiza. Olly had hated it but the TV experience would be useful. He was glad to be back at Divine Diva and working with Becky. He had wept with relief when Becky regained consciousness; he had held her hand in the hospital, as soon as she could have visitors and her parents had returned to Leeds. Olly had told her he was sorry if he had done anything to encourage Brookings and wanted her forgiveness. Becky told him there was nothing to forgive and she very much needed Olly to work with her, if he could live with the fact she saw dead people. Olly had told her he was only interested in the living, especially her. He had smiled as he kissed her cheek. Their eyes had locked, and Olly continued to hold Becky's hand as she smiled at him.

Sarah was waiting in the pale-green reception area of the Cube. Her outfit was a cream lace sack of a dress, slightly water-stained at the hem and wafting dampness. She wore huge silver hoops in her ears. She fussed over Becky when she arrived as if she were a fragile creature to be mothered.

Sarah pointed to a parcel, which had been delivered earlier that day. It was a slim box, almost two square metres. The label was ornately handwritten, copperplate, with Becky's name, and addressed to her at the Cube. There was no postal mark, no delivery paperwork. 'That came for you.'

Becky had been sent many gifts and cards during her recovery and she assumed that this was just another. Sarah picked up the box and told Becky that she was not to lift so much as a pen, after all she'd been through. She carried the parcel upstairs in the lift to the production office where Olly was waiting.

'What on Earth's that?' he asked, as Sarah propped the box up on his desk.

'A gift, I suppose,' said Becky. She took a pair of scissors and scored the cardboard box along the top in one fluid motion, the sound a satisfying rip. Then she scored the box down each side, curious to see what was inside. She peeled back the top corner.

A dark ebony, wood-carved, furled rose could be seen at the top corner of an antique mirror. Becky recognised it immediately, remembering how it had once unfurled, dropping black ichor as the faded glass had turned black. With a flash of fear, she ripped away the rest of the box and stepped back.

'Oh, Christ,' said Olly.

As they both looked at the mirror, last seen in York, Becky saw a single handprint, small but distinct, beginning to take shape, forming itself inside the glass.

TO BE CONTINUED

Thank you for reading *Medium Wave*

We hope you enjoyed it and would consider leaving a review of the book or a rating. It means so much to authors and publishers to get feedback about our books, so we can improve them and keep delivering books you love. All our books are professionally edited and proofread by our editorial team, however, occasionally a mistake might slip through. If you do find something, we hope that this would not spoil your enjoyment of the book but please make a note of it and send the details through to info@caffeinenights.com and we will amend it and ensure we give you something in return for your efforts.

Caffeine Nights Newsletter

If you would like to know more about the next Rose Zolock book or any of our other authors or books please sign up for our free newsletter at www.caffeinenights.com. Your email address and details are completely safe with us and never passed on or sold to anyone else and there is an unsubscribe link in every email should you choose you no longer want to receive our newsletter. All new newsletter subscribers can download a free eBook too.

We love social media and tweeting or posting on Facebook or putting a pic on Instagram is a great way to tell folks what you have enjoyed. You can follow us at:

Twitter: @caffeinenights

Facebook: CaffeineNights

Instagram: @caffeinenights

And if you share anything about our books we will share with our followers.